A Matter of Trust

GINNY WILLIAMS

HARVEST HOUSE PUBLISHERS
Eugene, Oregon 97402

A MATTER OF TRUST

Copyright © 1994 by Ginny Williams
Published by Harvest House Publishers
Eugene, Oregon 97402

Library of Congress Cataloging-in-Publication Data

Williams, Ginny, 1957–
    A matter of trust / Ginny Williams.
        p.   cm. — (Class of 2000 ; bk. 2)
    Summary: Although God has changed her heart, sixteen-year-old Kelly still finds it difficult to adjust to her father's remarriage, but when her beloved horse almost dies it is Kelly's stepmother who becomes a source of support.
    ISBN 1-56507-207-3
    [1. Remarriage—Fiction.   2. Horses—Fiction.
    3. Christian life—Fiction.]   I. Title.   II. Series:
Williams, Ginny, 1957–   Class of 2000 ; bk. 2.
PZ7.W65919Mat   1994   93-39060
[Fic]—dc20   CIP
                                                                    AC

Printed in the United States of America.

94 95 96 97 98 99 00 — 10 9 8 7 6 5 4 3 2 1

To Leann—
my best friend
and the great "wall-buster"
in my life

O N E

Kelly waved goodbye to her stepmother, Peggy, and her sister Emily, as they pulled away from the curb at Kingsport High. Her coppery curls glistened under the early morning sun and her wide blue eyes shone with anticipation as she turned to meet the excited crowd of fellow students who surged around her.

"Hello, Miss Celebrity! Can I have your autograph?"

"It's Kelly Marshall, the firefighter of the year!"

"I saw your picture in the paper. Weren't you scared to death when you went into that burning barn?"

"The school paper needs a good story. Can I do an interview on you and Crystal, the wonder horse?"

Kelly laughed helplessly and raised her hands in mock surrender. "Hey, you guys! What I did was no big deal. Any of y'all would have done the same thing. And, yes, I was scared to death, but I didn't really have time to think about it. Crystal was in that barn, and I wasn't about to let her get hurt or killed."

The admiring comments and jokes continued as the group moved toward the main entrance of the high school. It had been just three weeks since the big fire at Camp Sonshine. Kelly spent the summer at the North Carolina mountain camp working as a horse wrangler. Just a week before camp was to end, an awful fire destroyed the camp barn. Quick thinking and bravery on Kelly's part saved the three horses trapped in the barn. They would have died without her intervention.

One of the horses had been her own beloved Crystal, a beautiful coal-black filly given to the camp that summer. Kelly's love for the horse had forged a bond between her and Crystal that precluded anyone else. On her own, Kelly had tamed and trained her. To thank her for her act of bravery, the camp had given Crystal to Kelly. The spirited black filly was now safely stabled at Porter's Riding Stables, just minutes from her house.

The babble of voices continued around her as the students poured into the main mall area of the high school. It was the first day of her junior year, and just turned sixteen-year-old Kelly felt that life was perfect. Just before discovering the fire, she had finally quit fighting Jesus Christ and had given her life to him. She was getting along better with Peggy Marshall, her stepmother of four months. Her dream horse was even now roaming the lush green pastures at the stables. And to top it all off, her relationship with Greg Adams had definitely taken a turn for the better. Spending the summer with him at Camp Sonshine had been too good to be true.

As though beckoned by her thoughts, Greg's teasing voice came from over her right shoulder. "Quite the little celebrity, aren't you? Is it possible for me to break into this cozy group?"

Kelly flashed a brilliant smile at him and slipped her arm though his. The easy familiarity of their friendship still thrilled her. "Oh, I guess there's room since it's you. I was wondering if you would make it on time today. I figured at least one of your three little sisters would have a disaster that would make you late."

"Lacy threw a fit because she couldn't find her favorite horsie lunch box, but Mom finally unearthed it out in the garage. I guess when you're starting first grade, those things are pretty important." Greg laughed easily as he looked down in admiration at Kelly. "Not only are you a celebrity, but you look pretty great, too."

Kelly flushed under his warm approval. She had spent hours shopping with Peggy before she had found the soft blue jumpsuit she had chosen for the first day of school. Peggy had assured her the jumpsuit did a wonderful job of complementing her blue eyes and the golden tan she had acquired during the hours outside at Camp Sonshine. Evidently, Peggy had been right.

As she and Greg separated from the crowd and moved toward their first-period classes, she glanced up in admiration. Greg's lean, toned body looked great in his standard blue jeans. A bright red shirt contrasted against his deep tan. A pair of eyes as startlingly blue as Kelly's shone beneath his short, wavy, dark hair. It was his smile, though, that took her breath away every time he flashed it in her direction.

Greg shifted his books as he came to a halt outside her algebra class. "I've heard Mrs. Johnson is a tough algebra teacher, but she's supposed to be fair. I've got her for fifth period, so you'll have to give me the rundown at lunch. I'm bummed we don't have any classes together this semester, but at least we have the same lunch period."

"I'm glad for that, too. Algebra should be okay. Math is a pretty good subject for me. It's French that will do me in. I have hatchet-face Grimsley again this year. I'm sure she'll start nailing me for not being able to roll my R's any better now than I could at the end of last year. By the end of third period with her, I'm sure I'll be ready for some friendly lunch company."

Kelly raised her voice to continue as the first bell rang. "Your turn with Grimsley is coming this afternoon. I have to tell you, you're no better at rolling your R's than I am."

"Not only that, but the whole idea of male and female nouns is still ridiculous to me," he laughed. "Maybe we'll go to France together one day and be glad she hammered us over the head with all this stuff. See you later." Greg flashed his easy smile and moved off into the crowd.

Kelly gazed after his tall form until it disappeared around the corner. She walked into her class in a daze. *Maybe we'll go to France together one day!* Things were sounding better and better. Greg had still not kissed her, but Kelly was certain that she was special to him. Slipping into her seat, she stared dreamily out the window.

Voices penetrated her thoughts as others filtered into the room.

"That's Kelly Marshall! She had her picture in the paper for saving three horses out of a burning barn." Heads turned toward her at the words whispered from the back of the room.

Kelly wondered how long it would take for the talk to die down. She had to admit she was enjoying it. It was fun to be a hero, even if she didn't really feel like one. Her dad had laughingly commented that he hoped her head wouldn't swell so big today from all the compliments that she wouldn't be able to fit through the front door that night. To Kelly's way of thinking, the fall was sure to be pretty mild after the adventures of the summer. Her head wouldn't stay big for long.

"Hey, Kelly! I read about you in the paper. What you did was pretty incredible. Your horse looks pretty awesome, too."

Kelly turned toward her friend Julie. "Thanks. And you're right—Crystal *is* awesome. I still can't believe she's actually mine."

Julie gave her a sly smile. "I hear that's not all you got out of this summer."

Kelly was puzzled. "Huh?"

"The grapevine tells me you and Greg have turned into quite an item."

Kelly flushed but grinned. "Well, things are going pretty well. But we're just friends."

"Oh, sure. *I* don't have any friends who walk me to class and stare down at me while they're telling me how great I look." Julie laughed at Kelly's red face. "I was behind you when he walked up to you this morning. I'm not surprised you didn't see me. After he showed up, I don't think you saw anyone!"

"Okay, okay!" Kelly laughed. "Sure, I think he's pretty great. But we really are just friends."

Kelly searched for a way to change the subject. She liked Julie a lot, but she didn't really want to talk about Greg with her. "Hey, I thought I saw you with some guy in the hall. Who was he?"

"Oh, that's Brent. We've just started hanging out together. He called me last week, and we went to the movies. He's nice and I like him. I guess time will tell what happens." Julie paused for a moment. "Do you like to water ski?" she finally asked.

Kelly's face lit up. "You bet I do! I don't get to do it a lot, but I love it. One of Dad's real estate agents has a boat up on Lake Norman, and he used to take us. It's really fun."

Julie nodded in agreement. "I love it, too. My folks bought a boat this spring. We go skiing a lot now. Would you like to go sometime? Wouldn't it be fun to invite Brent and Greg and spend a day on the water? We could even have a cookout on the beach after we're done."

Kelly nodded her head vigorously. "I would love to do that. Just let me know when you think it might work out. I'll mention it to Greg."

"Well, it will need to be in the next few weeks. Once October hits, the water starts to get cold and it usually rains more. We'll fit it in while it's still nice. I'll let you know. I just need to talk to my folks." Julie reached down to pick up her notebook. "Are you going to Fall Bash?"

"I sure am. It sounds like fun. Getting Crystal was not the only cool thing that happened this summer, and Martin has asked me if I'll talk some about it.

I'm scared to death to get up in front of the group to talk, but I do want everyone to know what happened."

"I'll be there for sure. You'll really love it. It's the first time all the kids from church will be together since school was out." Julie's voice was drowned out as the last bell rang for class.

Kelly turned toward the front of the room just as Mrs. Johnson started to talk. The first day of class was always pretty easy. As Mrs. Johnson explained her expectations for the year, Kelly glanced out of the corner of her eyes to see who was sitting around her. Julie was on her right and Bernie, a casual friend from the year before, occupied the seat in front of her. Seated at her left was Michelle, a girl she didn't know well but was sure she would like if she had the chance to spend time with her.

As Mrs. Johnson droned on about algebra, Kelly's face flushed as she remembered Julie's teasing comments about Greg. Part of her had wanted to tell Julie how exciting her friendship with him was, to tell her how much she liked him and how much she dreamed of being his girlfriend. Why hadn't she? She knew other girls laughed and exchanged secrets, hopes, and dreams. Why couldn't she? She and her mom used to talk like that. When her mom died of cancer five years ago, that part of Kelly had died, too. Now she just locked away her thoughts and feelings. Kelly mentally shrugged and focused her attention on what her algebra teacher was saying. She was comfortable with the way she was. She didn't have to be like other girls.

"Open house for parents and students will be in two nights. I look forward to meeting with some of your parents. I'm sure you'll encourage them to come see me since math is your favorite subject." Mrs. Johnson laughed easily as groans rose from around the room. "Let's finish looking at the syllabus and test schedule for the fall." More groans followed that remark, but once again Kelly was lost to her thoughts. She could read the syllabus later.

Open house for parents... Kelly's recent relationship with Christ had allowed her to accept her new stepmother, Peggy. Peace now reigned in what had been an open battlefield in their home, but Kelly still struggled with her feelings. She accepted Peggy as her father's new wife, but where exactly was she supposed to fit into Kelly's life? What did Peggy expect from her? What did her father expect from her? What did God expect from her? This morning had been especially difficult. For the last five years her father had brought her to school, but today she rode with Peggy. The special relationship she and her father had shared since her mother's death seemed to have lessened since Peggy entered his life. Kelly supposed she could understand it, but it didn't make it any easier to accept.

The bell rang but Kelly, wrapped up in her thoughts, didn't even hear it.

"Hey, surely you don't like algebra so much you're going to stay for another period."

Kelly glanced up in confusion at Julie. Only then did she notice the quickly emptying room. Her face reddened, but she managed a casual laugh as she gathered her books. "Guess I was in outer space somewhere. It always takes me a few days to convince my brain that it has to go into school mode again."

"Especially when you have someone as good-looking as Greg to occupy your thoughts," Julie teased her again good-naturedly.

Kelly tried to respond as lightly, "Can you blame me?"

"Not a bit!" Julie gave her a grin as they reached the door.

As Kelly headed down the hallway, she was met with the familiar refrain of congratulations and teasing that had been with her all morning. Thoughts of Peggy and her father fled from her mind as she laughingly returned the comments. Greg would be waiting for her after French to go to lunch, and then they would be spending the afternoon at the barn. The problem with Peggy would work itself out.

TWO

Kelly peered through the dusty windshield of Peggy's car in order to inspect the fields looming up on her left. They were approaching the drive for Porter's Riding Stables. Most afternoons, Crystal was grazing on the lush pastures and enjoying the summer sun. Straining her eyes, Kelly was finally able to locate the filly's black form next to the stream under some sheltering trees. September could sometimes be the hottest month of North Carolina summers. This year would surely be in the record books. A very hot spring had evolved into an even hotter summer.

"C-r-y-y-y-s-t-a-a-a-l!" Kelly stretched her head out of the rolled-down window to call her beloved filly.

Immediately she saw the black filly's head shoot up and swerve in the direction of the car as it turned in the entrance gate to the stable. Moments later Crystal's magnificent body shot out of the woods as she headed for the gate where she always met her mistress. Kelly settled back with a sigh of satisfaction.

"I still marvel at the love that animal has for you. It's as if you've been together for years, not just a few months." Peggy laughed in admiration as she stopped the car in front of the stable clubhouse.

"I'm sure Crystal knows she is a dream come true for me. She loves me so much because I love her so much! It's pretty simple, really." Kelly spoke with the exuberance that always characterized her words about the filly. Opening the door, she stuck one leg out.

"Your dad will be by to pick you and Greg up on his way home from the office this evening. He has a late house showing, so he won't be able to get here until seven. I've packed you some fruit to keep you going until dinner tonight."

"Thanks, Peggy. I'm always happy for any extra time I can have out here. Crystal is learning so fast, and there is so much I want to teach her. Besides, I guess I can suffer through more time with Greg..."

Peggy shoved Kelly out of the car door as she tossed out her last laughing words.

"I'm sure you'll manage to endure it somehow," Peggy said with a wry smile. "Now get going. You have a very impatient filly waiting for you."

As if in response to Peggy's words, Crystal started bobbing her head over the pasture gate and nickering. Kelly ran to her and, after giving her shiny muscular neck a big hug, fed her the carrot Crystal was nosing her pockets for. "Honestly, I don't know if you love me or just the carrots I supply you with."

Crystal nickered as if to say *both* ingredients were important to the special relationship they shared.

Kelly looked up at the sound of pounding hooves. When she saw Shandy, Greg's beautiful buckskin gelding, flying across the field, she knew Greg must be coming in the gate. Sure enough, moments later he was waving goodbye to his mother as she pulled away from the clubhouse.

Greg joined her just as Shandy's head popped over the gate beside Crystal's. The two horses had become fast friends in the three weeks they had known each other. Greg produced the expected apple as he stroked his gelding's nose. "I know I've said this a hundred times before, but I sure am glad I was able to move Shandy out here to Porter's. The Lazy B Stable was okay, but it wasn't nearly as nice as this place. And besides, it's so much more fun to ride with you than alone."

Kelly thrilled at Greg's words as she agreed. "It's worked out just right for everyone—us *and* our horses. Let's go in and saddle up. I know it's miserably hot, but I still want to ride."

Greg turned to her eagerly. "I had a great idea in French today. I must admit Grimsley didn't have me hanging on her every word, so I was thinking about this afternoon. Let's ride bareback. Take them swimming in the lake! I think it'll be fun for all of us."

Kelly's words were a little hesitant. "It sounds great, but I've never done it before. Do you think Crystal will be okay?"

"Are you kidding? That filly will do anything for you. Besides, she'll love it. So will you. I promise."

• • •

Crystal needed no urging to follow Shandy into the cool, inviting waters. But as they moved deeper, she turned her head and eyed Kelly as if to question whether she was really doing what her mistress wanted. Kelly urged her on with her legs and watched Greg carefully so she could imitate his every move.

Just as Shandy's powerful legs lost contact with the lake bottom and began to stroke out like powerful pistons, Greg allowed his legs to float back. Still holding the reins loosely in his hands, he grabbed on to the buckskin's mane and laughed as he was pulled through the water.

Crystal tossed her head in joy as she felt the water buoy her body. Kelly let loose an exuberant yell at the feeling of freedom and coolness as she allowed her body to float. Crystal surged forward until she and Shandy were neck to neck. Kelly and Greg exchanged looks of delight as their laughter rang in the afternoon air.

Curious horses gathered around the edge of the lake to inspect the odd spectacle, but none ventured to join them. Riders in the teaching rings gazed over the ring railing in envy and dreamed of the day they could do the same.

Back and forth and in and out they went, with great splashings and sprays of water until everyone had their fill. Horses and people were all tired, but no one was hot—quite a feat in the sultry heat.

Choosing a favorite trail, Kelly and Greg reined the horses into the sheltering woods. The towering oaks and maples were the solid, dark green of late summer. Gazing through the thick canopy, Kelly could see tiny green scuppernongs. In another month or so, the fruit would be great clumps of purple grapes, and she would be picking them for Peggy to make scuppernong jelly—her dad's favorite. Silence enveloped them, and Kelly allowed her thoughts to wander.

Just four months ago she had been cleaning stalls, babysitting, and doing any odd job available in an effort to earn money for her dream horse. She could hardly believe the quiet animal she now rode through the shadows was the same frightened animal that had exploded from the trailer at Camp Sonshine just three months ago. Crystal was a long way from the five thousand-acre Texas ranch she had grown up wild on. From the beginning, Kelly and Crystal had shared a special love. Kelly had been truly amazed when the camp gave her Crystal in appreciation for saving the other horses in the fire. Her saved money had gone to buy all her tack and grooming supplies. She was still teaching classes to pay for her board, but cleaning stalls was a thing of the past.

Reaching down to absently pat Crystal's neck, Kelly thought about home. Things had changed so much since...

"Penny for your thoughts."

Kelly smiled at Greg's words. "Since my thoughts are about Crystal, I think they're probably worth a whole lot more. I was thinking about home, too. And about how much I've changed. Sometimes I can't believe I resented Peggy and Jesus Christ so much. Ever since I asked Jesus into my life, I just feel so different about things. I really like Peggy and am glad she and Dad are so happy..." Kelly hesitated, and Greg, regarding her closely, picked up the conversation.

"Sounds like there's a 'but' there somewhere. You really like Peggy, *but* ..."

Kelly was startled at Greg's perception. How had he known what she was thinking? She struggled with her response. "I don't know that there's a 'but.' It's just that it's hard to get used to all of the changes..." Her voice trailed off uncertainly.

"Anything in particular?"

Kelly glanced at Greg and was struck by the caring look on his face. Part of her yearned to tell him the truth, to tell him she was afraid to allow Peggy to get close, afraid to risk losing someone else she loved. But the words just wouldn't come. Her feelings had been locked up inside for too long. She would think through everything and come up with some answers on her own. She forced herself to laugh lightly. "No, nothing in particular. I know that it's going to take time for all of us to adjust. I just get impatient and want it to happen overnight."

Greg just nodded thoughtfully. "I'm really glad to know things are going so well. You seem to be a lot happier now."

"Oh, I am. There's really no way to describe the difference. Sometimes it is hard to be around other Christians, though. I feel so ignorant because I don't know the Bible very well. I'm afraid I'll sound really stupid if I open my mouth to say something or ask a question."

Greg laughed sympathetically. "Yeah, well only time can take care of that. Just remember, all of us started there. The important thing is wanting to learn and then doing something about it."

Kelly nodded in agreement and then lapsed into silence. Greg, sensing she didn't want to talk, said no more.

The air cooled as they slipped deeper into the woods. There were still some late-blooming wildflowers clamoring for attention on the side of the trails. Kelly contemplated how comfortable she felt with Greg. She knew people wondered if they were boyfriend and girlfriend. She also knew she was special to Greg and that they had drawn even closer since she had become a Christian, but they had never talked about their relationship. All in all, that was fine with Kelly. She had never been into people putting labels on everything. She and Greg were friends. They liked each other. They enjoyed being together. What did it matter what it was called? She had to admit that she daydreamed about the possibility of him kissing her, but she was happy with things as they were. She knew so many people who were considered boyfriend and girlfriend who were not nearly as good of friends as she and Greg.

Out of the corner of her eye, Kelly saw Greg studying her. Noticing her glance, he grinned but remained silent.

Kelly smiled in return. "I guess I'm being pretty quiet today. I just have so much to think about. The last three weeks have been pretty crazy with getting Crystal settled and getting ready for school. This seems to be the first peaceful day I've had in weeks."

"I don't mind your being quiet," Greg said. "I'm enjoying the peace, too. Nothing is better than being out here with Shandy like this. I'm glad I don't always have to be talking when I'm with you. Silence can be nice sometimes, too."

Kelly gave him a grateful look and said, "I think this year at school is going to be tough. I've heard from friends that your junior year is a hard one. I think some of my teachers are going to try to get me to self-destruct."

"You can say that again. Most seniors get in college during their first semester and decide they can lay back on the last semester. I guess the teachers figure they'll give it to us with both barrels loaded this year because so much depends on it. It's definitely going to be tough. School, church, and Shandy will pretty much take up all my time. Not to mention you. Say, have you seen the schedule for the church youth group this year? Martin and Janie have some pretty great things planned."

Reaching the end of the trail, they reined Crystal and Shandy around and started back toward the barn. Settling back on Crystal's broad, smooth back, Kelly replied, "I haven't seen the schedule, but I know about Fall Bash. I'm really looking forward to it. Is it something they do every year?"

"Yeah. Martin has always said that the people in this church are always on the go—especially during the summer. Anyway, Fall Bash is the first event of the new school year. Everybody is back, and I'm told they have a great time. The best part is that it's free. Martin likes to do something to get the year off to a good start, and it sounds like he really goes all out. There will be food, music, games, competition." Greg paused and then said with a cocky grin, "If you're lucky, you'll be on my team. I plan on winning, you know."

Kelly wrinkled her nose at him and replied haughtily, "Well, you should just hope I *am* on your team, because if I'm not, you're going to crash and burn!"

"We'll see, my lady, we'll see. Time has a way of taking care of disputes like this. At least, that's what my dad always says."

The rest of the ride back passed in quiet contemplation. The shadows were deepening, and the late afternoon coolness was refreshing. The horses had long since dried. They were cool and relaxed when they arrived back at the barn.

Granddaddy Porter, the owner of the stables, was outside the barn when they rode up. He chuckled at them. "Looked like y'all were having a ball down there. I can remember when I was a kid, taking the horses swimming in the lake was one of my favorite things to do. Greg, that must have been your idea. No one has done that around here for as long as I can remember."

Greg confessed, "Where I come from in Texas, you look for any way possible to stay cool when summer is around. The horses loved it."

"You bet they did," Granddaddy laughingly agreed. "What horse wouldn't rather be in the water than running around in this heat? The class horses were so hot after the afternoon classes that we hosed all of them down to cool them off. I sure hope there'll be a break in this weather soon. The calendar says the summer is over, but someone forgot to tell Mother Nature."

Kelly slipped off Crystal's back. "The trail ride is still on, isn't it? I can hardly wait to really show Crystal off to all the boarders. And it's always so much fun. I can hardly believe I'll be riding my own horse this year."

"You'll get your chance to show off all right." Granddaddy slipped his arm around Kelly's waist and gave her an affectionate hug. "And you've got every right to want to show off. You have yourself a fine horse here, and how you got her would make anyone proud." He looked at her for a second and then continued, "I want you to know how impressed I am with the way you've handled all the fame and attention. I didn't think you would let it go to your head, and I was right."

Kelly ducked her head and flushed with embarrassment. She gave him a big hug and mumbled a quick thanks.

Grabbing her bucket of grooming equipment, Kelly went to work. Crystal curled her lip as Kelly worked the rubber currycomb in a firm circular motion. She followed it with a soft brush to bring out the shine and then finished off with a soft cloth that polished the filly's coat to an ebony sheen. A quick cleaning of the hooves finished her work.

Greg had cross-tied Shandy in another area of the corridor and finished up about the same time Kelly did. "These guys have certainly earned their dinner," he commented. "Not to mention the fact I'm starving, too. Let's put them in their stalls, and then how about if we attack the fruit Peggy gave you? We still have thirty minutes before your dad gets here. I think I'll probably faint from hunger if I don't eat something."

Kelly's growling stomach forced her to agree. Giving Crystal a hug and kiss, she released her into the stall. Seconds later the sound of the horses munching filled the air. Settling down in the sawdust outside of Crystal's stall, Kelly reached into the bag of fruit and handed Greg an apple and some grapes.

Silence reigned in the barn as they relaxed in the familiar atmosphere of grain, leather, and horse smells. Crystal and Shandy snuffled comments back and forth between their stalls. A deep peace settled over Kelly and Greg as they leaned back against the stalls.

"Hey, sleepyhead! Your dad is here."

Kelly looked up drowsily at Greg. "Did I fall asleep?"

"Either that, or you were temporarily comatose." Greg grinned as he reached down and hauled her up from the floor. Putting his arm around her waist, he steered her in the direction of her dad's car.

Kelly was wide awake now, but she managed to maintain a sleepy exterior. The feel of Greg's arm around her waist was too good to lose. Too soon they were at the car.

"Good evening, Mr. Marshall," Greg greeted Kelly's father as he slid into the back seat.

"Hi, Dad. Thanks for coming to pick us up. How did the house showing go?"

Scott Marshall smiled at his oldest daughter. "I think it went pretty well, honey. I'll know in a few days if they decide to take it." He paused to take a closer look and grinned. "You look pretty beat. Did y'all have fun today?"

The rest of the ride to Greg's centered around their swimming adventures and what had happened at school.

When Greg had jumped out of the car, Kelly's father turned to her. "Peggy said she enjoyed taking you to school today."

Kelly merely nodded. She could see him regarding her quizzically, but she didn't know what to say.

"Is everything okay, Kelly?"

Her first impulse was to nod and smile, but something deep inside urged her on. Struggling to sound casual, she confessed, "I guess I just missed you taking me this morning, Dad." As soon as the words were out, Kelly knew they had sounded cold. Her attempt to sound casual had sounded more like an accusation. She searched for something to say to take the sting away. "I appreciated her taking me, though."

Her father took a deep breath and just nodded. "I guess now is as good a time as any to tell you about my trip."

Kelly looked up, startled. "What trip?"

"I've decided to go ahead and attend the annual Real Estate Convention in Chicago this year. I had thought maybe I wouldn't go, but I've decided it will be best if I do. Peggy and I have talked about it. She's excited about having some time with you girls alone."

Kelly's thoughts spun. Her father's words upset her, but she wasn't sure why. "How long will you be gone?"

"Two weeks. The convention lasts a week, and then I'm going to stop and see your mom's parents on my way home."

Kelly flinched at the mention of her mom. Peggy's presence in the house was bringing up painful memories of her mother's death. Kelly was doing her best to avoid feeling them. "I see." Knowing she needed to say more, she added, "I know Grandma and Grandpa will be glad to see you. When are you leaving?"

"In a week. I wasn't sure I would be able to get a hotel reservation at this late date, but they had a cancellation and I was able to squeeze in."

"That's great, Dad." Kelly forced a warmth in her voice she wasn't feeling. She couldn't imagine what it was going to be like at home without her dad, but she would just have to make the best of it. Taking a deep breath, she smiled brightly at her father as they pulled into their driveway. "Here we are. Are you as hungry as I am?"

Hopping out of the car, they headed to the house together. Wonderful aromas assaulted Kelly's senses as they burst in the back door of their home.

"Good. You're right on time. This spaghetti casserole is best when it's served hot." Peggy turned from the oven to give Scott a kiss as he greeted her. "Emily, will you put the salads on the table and fill the tea glasses?"

Kelly's younger sister, Emily, moved to do as Peggy had requested. While Kelly was a female replica of her father, Emily was a tiny version of the mother they had lost to cancer five years earlier. Her long, blonde hair framed a heart-shaped face dominated by violet-colored eyes. At twelve years old, she already had her mother's easygoing temperament. Unlike Kelly, who had rebelled at her father's marriage, Emily had instantly adored Peggy. Yet in spite of their differences, Kelly and Emily were very close

Sitting down at the table, they all bowed their head for the blessing which Kelly's father asked in his rich, deep voice. Kelly shared about her day with Peggy and Emily, then Emily dominated the rest of the conversation with stories about school. Kelly was glad for a chance to be quiet. She was listening to her sister but she was also becoming more aware of how exhausted she was. It had been a long, full day, and she was looking forward to her bed. Thankfully, none of her teachers had assigned homework on the first day of classes.

"Kelly, why don't you be excused and go upstairs before your face falls into what's left of your spaghetti?"

Kelly smiled gratefully at Peggy as she pulled her weary body from the table. "Thanks. I *am* pretty beat. The meal was great, but I'm just too tired to finish. I'm going to take a shower and call it a night."

• • •

A little while later, Kelly was crawling into bed when she realized she had almost forgotten to have her quiet time. She hadn't even known what a quiet time was until Martin had asked if she was having one. Martin had said it was really important to spend time reading the Bible and praying every day. She sometimes forgot, but she was honestly trying to make it a habit. Kelly never did things halfway, and she really wanted to grow as a Christian and know God better.

Reaching over to flip her light back on, Kelly picked up the Bible that sat on her nightstand. Martin had suggested she start with the book of John, and she was now on the thirteenth chapter. Verse 34 seemed to jump out at her as she read: "A new command I give you: Love one another. As I have loved you, so you must love one another. By this all men will know that you are my disciples, if you love one another." Peggy's face floated into Kelly's mind.

But God, Kelly's thoughts protested, *it's not that I don't love Peggy, or that I'm choosing not to. I think I'm just afraid to love her too much. I know she's a neat person, but what if I lose her, too? I don't think I could handle that. I'm doing okay the way I am.*

Having convinced herself she could play the game the way she wanted to, Kelly rolled over and immediately fell asleep.

THREE

Kelly reached over and slapped the offending alarm clock. "Oh, shut up!" She rolled over to bury herself under the covers again, but Emily bounded through the door.

"Hey, Kelly! Time to rise and shine. Peggy sent me to remind you we have to leave about fifteen minutes early this morning. She has a house showing to do for Dad."

Kelly groaned and threw the covers back. "Yeah. Okay. I'll be ready. Who appointed you little Miss Sunshine, anyway?" The tenseness she had been feeling since her father left was evident in her voice.

Emily disappeared out the door, but not before Kelly saw the hurt expression on her face. Kelly flung her legs over onto the floor and sighed. Her father had left the day before for his convention, and Kelly was struggling with her feelings about living with Peggy without her father around. It made Peggy seem too much like a mom, and Kelly wasn't ready for that. Walking over to her window, she breathed in deeply and knew the weatherman had been right. A cold front had blasted through

31

last night, dropping the temperatures and giving them their first cool day in months. Riding that afternoon would be awesome, but first she had to get through Peggy and school.

• • •

"Hey, Kelly."

Kelly glanced up as Julie took her seat next to her in algebra. "Give me a minute," Kelly said. "I need to finish up this last problem. I fell asleep last night before I could figure it out."

Julie made a wry face. "At least you can figure it out. This stuff is like Greek to me. I have come to accept that I don't have a mathematician's mind. I stayed up until midnight working on these problems, but I only got through half of them."

Kelly looked up and smiled. "This stuff is pretty easy for me. Would you like some help sometime?"

Julie grinned. "I thought you'd never ask. I've watched you whip through those things and wanted to ask you for help, but you're always so busy. When would you have time?"

"I'm sure we can work it out." Kelly was warmed by the look of appreciation on Julie's face. The more she got to know Julie, the more she realized she really wanted a good friend. She wondered that it had never seemed important before.

The bell rang, and everyone hurried to take their seats. Julie leaned over and whispered, "Save Brent and me a seat at lunch. We need to talk about our waterskiing trip. Looks like a week from Sunday is it."

Kelly nodded and then turned her attention to Mrs. Johnson. Algebra came pretty easy to her, but she still had to listen and study. She knew her junior year was important if she was going to get into a good college.

The rest of the morning flew by. Her head was pounding when she walked out of French. They'd only been in school a week, and already hatchet-face Grimsley was giving them impossible tests. Kelly had studied hard for it, but she couldn't tell how she'd done.

"Looks like you're ready for some lunch." Greg grinned sympathetically as he walked up to her. "It was that bad, huh? If you had that much trouble, I'm sunk for sure. Are there any particular areas I need to bone up on before I take it?"

"Yeah. *Every* area." Kelly rolled her eyes and smiled ruefully. "No one can accuse Grimsley of being a cream-puff teacher. If I survive her class, I am definitely going to France. There has to be some reason I'm suffering through such abuse."

Greg laughed. "Let's go get some lunch. Brent asked me to save a seat for him and Julie."

"Julie asked me the same thing. Said they wanted to make plans for the ski trip. Julie mentioned something about a week from Sunday."

"Sounds good to me. We'd better go before fall has hung around too long. That water can get pretty cold."

Kelly and Greg picked up burgers and fries from the lunch line. They definitely looked better than the unidentifiable mass that was supposed to be broiled fish.

"How are things going with your dad gone?"

Kelly didn't know how to answer Greg. It was hard for her to be with Peggy without her father around, but she didn't really understand it herself. "Oh, it's okay. Dad's only been gone since yesterday afternoon."

Just then Julie's voice sounded above her head. "Is it okay if we join the cozy twosome?"

Greg grinned easily and waved them toward the other two seats at the table. "Help yourself. Anyone who wants to take me waterskiing is a friend of mine!"

Kelly grinned in agreement as Julie and Brent settled in at the table. Julie's blonde hair and laughing blue eyes lit up a face that was attractive because of the life and fun that welled up within her. Julie was one of the most popular girls at school, but it didn't seem to affect her. Brent was only an inch or two taller than Julie's 5' 6" frame, but he had the build of an athlete. Last year he had been voted most valuable player on the school soccer team. His curly brown hair and eyes were deepened by a tan he seemed to keep all year long. From what Kelly could tell, he was friendly but extremely quiet.

"Did Kelly tell you about the ski trip, Greg?" Julie asked as the four of them ate their lunch.

"She did. It sounds great! She said something about the Sunday after Fall Bash. Are you wanting to head up after church?"

"Yes. That should give us plenty of time for several hours of skiing and then a cookout on the beach. It doesn't get dark until about eight."

"Sounds like fun to me!"

Kelly and Brent echoed his words. The four of them spent the rest of lunch making plans, deciding who would bring what and how they would manage transportation.

A few minutes before the bell rang, Greg stood and looked down at Kelly. "Are you ready? I've got something I want to show you."

Kelly looked at him quizzically, but he just grinned. Nodding, she told Brent and Julie goodbye and rose to join Greg. "Where are we going?"

"Oh, I just want to show you something."

Walking down the hallway, he led her to the entrance of the gym. "There."

Kelly gazed around. "What? All I see are some kids putting up a sign."

"Exactly."

Kelly was confused. "Excuse me if I sound dense, but what exactly is the purpose of bringing me to see some kids putting a sign up?"

Greg sighed and tried to sound patient. "What does the sign *say?*"

Kelly moved a little closer and read the words brightly painted on the long banner:

GET YOUR TICKETS NOW FOR
THE FALL HOMECOMING DANCE
OCTOBER 10 • 8:00—11:00

She finished reading and then waited with bated breath. Could it mean what she thought it meant?

"So. What do you think?" Greg asked.

"What do I think about *what?*" Kelly was getting frustrated.

Greg finally laughed. "Okay, I'm doing a lousy job of this. Sorry. This is my first time to ask a girl to a dance. I'd really like to take you. Will you go with me?"

Kelly turned to him with shining eyes. "I'd love to, Greg...and it will be my first dance, too."

"No way! I figured you'd been to lots of these things."

"I was always too much into horses and being at the barn." Kelly added shyly, "I think it will be a lot of fun with you, though."

Greg grinned. "I guess it's a good thing we'll be there. The school doesn't know what it's been missing."

Kelly didn't trust her voice, so she didn't say anything else as he walked her to her next class.

• • •

Kelly drew in a deep breath of cool, fresh air as Crystal nosed her pockets for carrots. The clouds in the overcast sky had been blown away by a strong breeze. The first cool air to hit North Carolina in months washed over her body. Crystal pranced as if to indicate her approval of the invigorating change in temperature. Shandy poked his nose over the gate beside his ebony friend, making Kelly laugh.

"Sorry, boy. Greg had to work this afternoon, so you're on your own. He didn't forget you, though. I know you'd rather have him, but an apple will have to suffice." Reaching in her pocket, she pulled out the apple Greg had given her. Shandy nodded his head as if to say it was better than nothing.

"Let's go, Crystal. We've got a beautiful afternoon and a lot of work to do."

Kelly had made arrangements with Mandy, her friend as well as Granddaddy's trainer and instructor, to work with her and Crystal for an hour. She didn't want to waste a single minute of it.

Twenty minutes later, freshly groomed and tacked up, Crystal emerged from the barn with Kelly leading her. Arching her neck and holding her head proudly, she pranced toward the large teaching ring. Kelly's heart swelled with pride at the sight of her magnificent animal. Crystal was everything she had dreamed of and more.

Kelly knew she had twenty minutes before Mandy was to join them. She spent that time walking and trotting Crystal at an easy speed so all of her muscles would be loose and warm. They were ready when Mandy climbed on top of the rail with a friendly wave.

"Y'all look ready for anything."

Kelly rode up to where her friend sat. "You bet we are. I really appreciate your taking some time to work with us."

"Hey, as many times as you worked Granddaddy's horses with me this spring, I'd be downright selfish if I didn't!" She continued with an open smile, "Besides, it's fun to see how fast the two of you are learning. You were definitely made for each other."

Hitching her legs under the railing, Mandy motioned Kelly to take Crystal to the outer rail of the ring. "We're going to work on Crystal's canter today. We already know it's incredibly smooth, but she needs some work on taking the right lead. When she's doing ring work or showing, it will be really important. If she's not leading off on that inside leg, she'll be thrown off balance going into the curves and turns. It's an inconvenience when you're just doing ring work, but judges will count off for it in shows. I want you to stay all the way to the outside. When you move into the far curve, I want you to move your outside leg just a little behind the girth while turning her head to the outside a little. When you ask her to canter, it should cause her body to naturally go into the correct lead."

Kelly knew that Crystal could sense her change in attitude. It was no longer time to relax; it was time to work. The filly's intelligent dark eyes flashed as she waited for direction. One ear was cocked back for Kelly's quiet command. As they moved into the curve, Kelly followed Mandy's directions and asked Crystal for a canter.

Crystal swung easily into a canter, but Kelly immediately pulled her back down into a walk. The filly glanced back in confusion.

"Try it again, Kelly," Mandy called. "Having grown up on an open range, Crystal is used to taking off on her stronger leg. Horses are right- and left-handed—or legged—just like we are. It seems more natural for her to start off on that outside leg."

Kelly patted the filly and murmured to her in an easy tone. She didn't want to upset her horse. She knew Crystal would do anything for her. She just had to give her time to understand what she wanted.

For the next hour they moved in and out of a canter, switching directions every few minutes. By the end of their time together, Crystal was choosing the correct leader over eighty percent of the time. Kelly was proud of her. With practice, Crystal would become more consistent.

"Good job, you two," Mandy congratulated the pair. "Would you like to come over for something to drink after you put Crystal away?"

"Can we play that one by ear? I want to take Crystal on the trails for a while so that she doesn't get ring sour. All work and no play..." Letting her voice trail off, Kelly unlatched the gate and led the still-eager horse through. "If I have enough time when I'm done, I'll come by."

"I'll be there. I've already put all the horses' dinners in their feed buckets. I'm going to get my own food started."

As Kelly moved into the canopy of trees sheltering the trail, she relaxed her reins and legs to see if Crystal was ready for a rest. Crystal shook her head in disagreement, snorted, and pranced a few feet sideways to indicate she wasn't the least bit tired. They had done their work; now she was ready to have some fun.

Kelly laughed in agreement, and they moved off at a smart trot through the woods. The cool air playfully tossed the leafy canopy and split the sun's rays into dancing particles of light on the trail. The early morning rain had washed the sky a brilliant blue. Both Kelly and Crystal felt like they were on top of the world.

Breaking out into the large open field, Crystal asked for her head. Leaning forward, Kelly yelled in delight as they flew across the pasture toward the tall oak on the far side. Horse and girl soared as one across the grassy terrain. Kelly was sure life couldn't get any better than this.

Having run herself out, Crystal was content to meander her way back toward the barn at an easy walk. Kelly was always sure Crystal was cool and dry before she put her away for the night. Putting her up hot or wet wasn't good for her—it would be too easy for her to get sick. Kelly was determined to give Crystal the very best care possible. She didn't know what she would do if something were to happen to her beloved filly.

· · ·

Cool air washed over Kelly as she curled up on the large window seat. As usual, she was exhausted by her long day, but she wasn't ready to relinquish the feel of the refreshing breeze on her body. It had been a long, hot summer. The tall oak sentinel standing guard by her window whispered joyfully of the approaching fall. Twinkling stars sang the song of the new season. The honeysuckle outside her second-story window had lost all its fragrant blooms, but the crisp, clean air needed no perfume. It was perfect the way it was. Kelly breathed in deeply, trying to draw peace into her heart. Dinner had been tense. She simply could not relax around Peggy.

"I was checking to see if you were asleep yet."

Kelly yawned sleepily and beckoned Peggy into the room. "Come on in. I should be in bed, but this night is too wonderful." Moving her legs back, she made room for her stepmother on the window seat.

In spite of her feelings, Kelly was trying to do the right things.

"Sounds like you have a lot going on in the next week or so."

"That's for sure. Saturday is the big trail ride, and then Sunday is Fall Bash. Next week I have a couple of big tests, and I've promised to help Julie with her algebra a couple of days right after school. Then next Sunday Greg and I are going waterskiing with Julie and Brent."

"Waterskiing? I haven't heard about this yet."

Kelly felt irritation creeping into her heart. She didn't have to explain her actions to Peggy. She knew it would be fine with her dad. Peggy wasn't her mom. She didn't have to act like it.

"Oh, Julie's folks have a boat down on Lake Norman." Kelly tried to sound casual. "The four of us are going to spend the afternoon skiing and then have a cookout on the beach."

"Do you think that's such a good idea? Sounds like you have a pretty full schedule."

"I can handle it just fine." Kelly knew her voice was short and hard.

Peggy hesitated. "Martin called me today," she finally said. "He said they were short on help for Fall Bash and asked me if I would come out. What do you think?"

Kelly knew Peggy was trying to be nice, but her heart was not able to respond to what her mind was telling her. "Whatever. I don't care if you're there or not."

The hurt on Peggy's face was obvious, but she kept her voice light. "All right. I'll give him a call in the morning and let him know I'll be there." Standing, she looked down at Kelly for a moment. Then with a "Good night," she walked from the room and gently closed the door.

Kelly felt sick at heart, but she was also struggling with anger. She was trying to be nice to Peggy. Why did she have to come up here and try to act like her mom? Why couldn't she just be her father's wife? Kelly felt so torn inside. Part of her wanted to talk to her stepmother the same way she had talked to her mom when her mom would find her perched on the window seat. Those times had been so special.

Sighing, Kelly picked up her Bible, switched on the light, and tried to read. The words swam before her eyes and nothing made sense. Why was she crying? Taking a deep breath, Kelly willed herself to control her emotions. Turning over, she drifted into a restless sleep.

FOUR

Kelly knew she was showing off, but she couldn't resist using Crystal in her demonstration of how to tack a horse. The eight young kids gathered around her were wide-eyed in their appreciation of her beautiful filly. Sensing she was the center of attention, Crystal had pranced and danced her way into the barn aisle where Kelly was going to show her class of intermediate students how to saddle and bridle their horses. Their speechless awe had apparently satisfied Crystal's need for approval because she had settled down to the mundane task asked of her. Her neck was arched proudly as if to assure the group Kelly was doing a wonderful job of tacking her up.

"How you put the tack on is very important," Kelly began. "I can see by the great job you've done that all of you have already learned how to groom your horses." The eight class horses they were going to ride in their lesson were cross-tied and lined up down the corridor. "How you put on their bridle and saddle are just as important, if not more so.

43

Let's start with the saddle. Actually, we'll be starting with the saddle pad."

Lifting the fleecy white pad from the stand where it rested, Kelly held it up for the kids' inspection. "Regular riding leaves the pads stained and matted from your horse's sweat. The matted fleecing hardens and eventually becomes uncomfortable to their backs. They can't tell you themselves, but your horses sure will appreciate it if you wash it occasionally. I do Crystal's every week. Any less often and your folks will probably make you take it down to the Laundromat instead of fouling up your own washing machine."

Chuck Jacobsen spoke up eagerly from his position in the front. "I remember when my mom and I saw you and Mandy in the Kingsport Laundromat doing the stable pads. What a mess! I didn't think those things would ever come clean!"

Chuck Jacobsen, along with his younger brother, Frank, were Kelly's two favorite students. She had moved them up from the beginner ring, where she had been teaching in the spring, just before she left for Camp Sonshine. She was glad to have them back now that she was teaching intermediate classes.

"They were pretty disgusting!" Kelly laughingly agreed. "There is not enough time around here to wash them weekly, so when they get done it takes a lot of soap and washing to get them clean. It's worth it, though."

Placing the pad on the now-quiet filly's back, Kelly continued with her instruction. "Before you lay the pad down, check for any burrs or sticks or anything caught in the fleece. When you lay the pad down, make sure it's flat. Wrinkles and lumps could cause real discomfort to your horse. He's doing a lot for you. The least you can do is make sure he feels good." Smoothing it out, Kelly demonstrated while she spoke.

"Now comes the hard part, at least for you smaller ones—getting the saddle on your horse. That's why you see the wooden boxes next to your horses. Standing on those should get you up high enough to do it." Lifting the saddle off the stand, Kelly held it up in the air where everyone could see. "Pull the right stirrup and the girth over the saddle so they won't flap around and hit or scare your horse." Kelly gently lifted the saddle onto Crystal's back. "Make sure the pad is smooth over the horse's back and that it covers the horse's withers. It's the area most easily rubbed. Once you have the saddle in place, go around to the other side and let down the stirrup and girth."

Working as she talked, Kelly showed the group how to position the girth and tighten it. "One of a horse's favorite tricks is to hold his breath while you are tightening his girth. When you finish, he lets his breath out, and all of a sudden that pesky girth is not nearly so tight. You go to get on and your horse laughs at you when you end up in the dirt because the saddle is hanging sideways on his body." The whole group giggled at Kelly's rueful expression.

Frank, Chuck's younger brother, spoke up. "You look as if it's happened to you before."

"More than once! I was always so eager to get on that I would often forget. It finally got through my head that falling on my bottom was not that much fun." Kelly laughed good-naturedly with the rest of the group.

"Okay, everyone, let's give it a try. We don't ride today until all the horses are tacked up right." Kelly spent the next fifteen minutes helping the eager students, giving advice and correcting mistakes. Finally she was satisfied. "Good job! Now, let's tackle the bridle. It's much smaller than the saddle, but it can be more difficult if your horse decides, *No, thank you, I don't care for any metal to eat today!*"

Kelly demonstrated the correct position of the bridle. "Always make sure your reins are over your horses' necks before you untie them and take the halters off. Otherwise, you're going to have a very difficult time stopping them if they decide to take off." Kelly showed them the proper way to hold the bridle and how to use their thumbs in the back of their horses' mouths to force them to open their teeth. Crystal, always eager to go for a ride, opened her mouth before the bridle was halfway there. "Okay, well the *rest* of you will need to know that little trick. Crystal is a very easy demonstration horse."

It didn't take long for the rest of the horses to be bridled. Crystal stomped her foot indignantly when Kelly stripped off her tack and returned her to her stall. She clearly wanted to get on with it. Putting on saddle and bridle always meant they were going for a ride.

Kelly gave her a hug and whispered in her ear, "Don't worry, girl. Your turn is coming. Today is the day of the big trail ride. Right now I have to teach lessons. I'll be back."

Hurrying out to the ring where her class was warming up at a walk, she climbed onto the fence railing and breathed in deeply. The cool front was holding. It looked like fall was finally here. The air was crisp and clear, and all the horses were on good behavior. She could tell they appreciated the break in the weather as much as she.

Giving them several minutes to warm up, they spent the last thirty minutes of class working on the sitting trot. "Rhythm with your horse is a crucial part of good horsemanship," she instructed as the kids rode. "Some of y'all look like popcorn in a popper! The idea is to sit smoothly on your horse, not pound his back to death."

Jumping off the fence, she strode to where she had halted them. "Try this. How many of you know what a belly dancer is?" The kids giggled but nodded assent. "I want you to pretend you're a belly dancer. I want everything tight from your hips down. Grip tightly with your legs to maintain contact with your horse. From the hips up, I want you loose as a goose." Placing her hands on her stomach and back, she demonstrated moving her body to stay in rhythm with the horse. She smiled as the kids laughed but made sure they understood. She knew if they would listen, they would get it.

Turning around to return to her seat on the fence, she flushed red with embarrassment. Greg, barely able to control his laughter, was standing beside her spot.

"Greg! What are you doing here?"

"I came for my belly-dancing lesson. Am I too late?"

Kelly couldn't resist laughing as she took a swing at him. "I admit it looks silly, but it works."

"Yeah, well I just didn't expect to see my girl belly-dancing in the middle of a riding arena."

My girl! Kelly could barely control the quiver in her voice as she turned back to her class and tried to appear casual. "What *are* you doing here? I thought your dad had you working today."

"He had to go into town to buy some extra supplies, so he gave me an hour off. I thought I would surprise you and bring lunch." Grinning, he pulled a big box of chicken and biscuits from behind his back.

"How did you know I was starving?" Kelly's face glowed with delight at Greg's thoughtfulness.

"I'll be by the clubhouse when you get done with your class. See you in a few."

Kelly found it almost impossible to concentrate on the twenty minutes left in her class. Thankfully, all the kids had taken to heart her belly-dancing lesson and were doing much better as they worked on their sitting trots. Forcing her thoughts back to them, she called encouragement and gave small pointers. Finer aspects of form could wait. She was more interested in getting them to move as one with their horses.

• • •

Kelly washed the dust and dirt off her hands and face and then joined Greg where he waited at the picnic table beneath the towering oak.

"Thanks for bringing the food."

"You bet." He smiled. "I wasn't about to pass up an opportunity to see my girl and my horse all at the same time."

My girl again! Kelly tried to control her soaring emotions as she bit into the crispy chicken. Silence enveloped them until the last morsel had been picked from the box.

"So how are things going at home with your dad gone?" Greg asked.

Kelly carefully wiped her hands clean on the bounty of napkins Greg had packed in the box while her mind raced to come up with an answer. Why was he asking a question like that? she wondered. But why shouldn't he ask that question? She decided she was being paranoid. "Oh, they're okay. Why do you ask?"

Greg paused while he thought about his response. "I guess because you've seemed a little uptight the past couple of days, and I can't think of any other reason."

Kelly just stared at him. How could he have noticed she was tense? She thought she was doing a great job of covering it up—except for the one late-night conversation with Peggy, of course. But he had no way of knowing about that.

"Look, Kelly. Just because you became a Christian this summer doesn't mean everything in your life is going to immediately get better. I know you've accepted Peggy, but it still must be difficult having another woman in your house. I mean, from what you've told me, you and your mom were really close. Isn't it hard to figure out where Peggy fits into all that?"

Kelly sighed. "Yeah. It is hard. I'm really trying, but sometimes I just can't control myself. I want to do what's right. I want to do what God would want me to. I'm just having a hard time making sense of all of it. I'm afraid I'm blowing it."

Greg reached over and took her hand. "Give yourself time. God is certainly willing to do that. He doesn't expect perfection of you. He just wants you to try. He already knows you're going to blow it sometimes. He loves you anyway. All he wants to do is help you walk through it and learn the things you need to learn."

Kelly felt tears welling up in her eyes, but she took a deep breath and forced them back down. She didn't know why she was so constantly on the edge of losing control. She had never been like this, and she didn't like it. How could she tell Greg what she was feeling? She knew that if she didn't give her heart to someone, then she wouldn't have to worry about being hurt. It had taken her too long to get over her mother's death. She didn't want to go through agony like that again. She had finally learned how to protect her heart, and she wasn't willing to give that up.

She just nodded at Greg. There was no way she could express her feelings. They were racing through her mind, but she just couldn't bring herself to verbalize them.

Greg sensed their conversation was over. He looked at his watch, tossed the chicken box into the trash can, and stood up to stretch. "I've got to be going. Dad needs me to finish the job he's doing in the garage, and I want to have plenty of time to get

Shandy ready for the trail ride. I used to be sure Shandy would steal the show anywhere I took him. Now I've got some pretty tough competition in that black filly of yours."

Kelly privately thought that not even Shandy held a candle to her beloved Crystal, but she didn't think it wise to say so. "The two of them together should knock everyone's socks off," she agreed. "Did you know Granddaddy was joining us tonight? He hardly ever rides anymore—says his bones can't take it—but he always joins us for the annual trail ride."

"It sounds great. I'll see you in a few hours."

• • •

Kelly used an hour after lunch to ride two new horses Granddaddy was trying out. Then she spent the remainder of the afternoon cleaning her tack and putting finishing touches on her filly's shiny coat. Both she and Crystal knew there was nothing she could do to add any more shine to the gleaming mass, but it gave Kelly an opportunity to lavish attention on her horse, and Crystal enjoyed every minute of it.

Kelly was glad she didn't have to spend every minute at the barn working like she used to in order to earn money to buy a horse. The most wonderful horse in the world was hers, and she was free to enjoy her. The three hours spent teaching every Saturday morning to pay for board were not work— they were fun.

Kelly could hear the others arriving as she finished tacking Crystal. She waited until she figured almost everyone was there before leading her prancing filly out into the paddock. Pausing at the gate, Kelly whispered into Crystal's ear, "You're the most beautiful horse in the world. I'm so proud I get to show you off to everyone."

Vaulting into the saddle, Kelly was pleased by the admiring looks thrown her way. Many of the people joining the trail ride tonight were not regulars, so they had not seen her stunning filly. All of them, though, had heard or read the story of how she got her. Kelly glowed as the air filled with comments and compliments.

"You'd better be careful. Granddaddy is going to have to take back his words about all the fame not going to your head. You're being a pure ham tonight!"

Kelly flushed as she turned at the sound of Greg's teasing voice. "I *am* being an awful ham. Isn't Crystal something, though?"

"I'd say that both of you are something." Greg fixed her with a steady look before turning and riding off to help an older woman with her horse.

Kelly flushed even redder at his comment. Greg sure was being open about his feelings for her lately, she thought. What did it all mean?

Her attention was diverted by one of the boarders riding up to comment on Crystal. Pushing away her thoughts about Greg, Kelly turned her attention to the crowd of horses and people milling around. She cheered along with the rest when Granddaddy rode from the barn on a tall, bay gelding he had just bought. It was one of the horses Kelly had ridden that afternoon. She knew his gaits were smooth and would be kind to Granddaddy's "old bones."

Kelly and Greg found themselves about halfway back in the pack of horses making their way across the pasture toward the woods. Granddaddy had secured passage on three neighboring farms so the trail ride would be good and long. They weren't due back for three hours.

"I heard the trail is going to take us along the river for a couple of miles."

Kelly stopped people watching to respond to Greg's comment. "That's right. It's one of my favorite parts. I wish we were free to ride there any time we want, but the man who owns it won't let us. Granddaddy talks him into it for the annual trail ride every time, though. Once we get past the river, there is a huge pasture where anyone who wants to can race." Kelly paused and then casually tossed out, "I plan on winning this year."

Greg eyed her with sympathy and snorted, "In your dreams! No one has a chance against Shandy."

"We'll see. We'll see."

Kelly and Greg grinned at each other in friendly rivalry. Each knew the other would do their best to win, and that was okay. Their friendship was too secure to be hurt by a horse race. It would be fun to find out which horse was the fastest.

The time flew by in pleasant talk with other trail riders. Before they knew it, the large, open "racing pasture" was before them. Only ten of the riders had stepped forward to participate in this year's contest. Friendly teasing ceased when Granddaddy rode his horse to the starting line. It was his job every year to launch the race. Kelly settled in low over Crystal's back and tossed a quick smile to Greg, who occupied the same position on his powerful buckskin. They were both sure the contest would ultimately be decided between their two horses.

After the whistle blew, it took only a few seconds for that truth to become reality. As soon as Kelly released the reins, Crystal sprung forward like a tightened coil. Leaning forward in her stirrups, Kelly hung low over her horse's neck and spoke to her in encouraging words. She was thrilled and a little frightened at the speed with which Crystal responded. Out of the corner of her eye, she could see Shandy maintaining a neck-to-neck position.

Halfway through the pasture, Kelly saw Shandy edge into the lead. She continued to speak to her filly, and the gap closed. Vaguely she was aware of shouts and calls coming from the rest of the trail riders, but as far as she was concerned, there was no one else but the four of them involved in this contest.

The large maple marking the end of the race loomed in Kelly's vision as Crystal and Shandy raced toward it. "Come on, girl," Kelly encouraged. "You can do it. I just know you're the fastest!" From somewhere Crystal called on more speed and surged to the front. The race ended with Crystal in the lead by just one stride.

Kelly was flushed with triumph as she brought Crystal down to a walk and turned back to the crowd. They were cheering and calling as she waved in victory and then hugged her winded filly's neck.

"I'll get you next time!"

Kelly laughed into Greg's smiling face. "Wasn't that great? It was so close!"

"You were really good. Crystal is sure one fast horse. But this isn't the end. In fact, it's just the beginning. Shandy and I will be back to regain our reputation."

"Crystal and I will take you on any time!"

The rest of the trail ride passed peacefully as they walked their horses to cool and relax them. The sun had dropped behind the trees, and the sky cast a rosy hue over the retiring day. Reaching behind her, Kelly untied her sweatshirt from her saddle and snuggled into the warmth it offered. Yes, fall was on the way.

"I don't know about you," Greg said as they neared the end of the trail ride, "but I'm starving!"

"Same here," Kelly agreed. "I sure am glad all the people back at the barn are going to have dinner ready for us when we get there."

"You can say that again. I can taste the burgers and chocolate chip cookies now. Make sure you go for the plate of cookies my mom fixed. They're the best in the state."

Kelly gave him a sly smile. "I guess that will give us something else to compete for!"

"No competing on this one. I made sure she fixed plenty."

Laughing, they rode into the barnyard. The rest of the evening passed in a blur of eating, talking, and having a good time. Kelly was thrilled when she was called forward to receive the stable trophy that went to the winner of the "pasture race" each year. Peggy and Emily cheered the loudest.

At the end of the evening, Kelly readily accepted Greg's offer of a ride home. They worked together to help the clean-up crew make the stables look like a big group had never been there.

As they finished, Greg said, "Let's go in and check on the horses before we head home. I'm sure they're fine, but I want to make sure Shandy isn't too depressed about losing the big race to two girls!"

Kelly laughed and punched him lightly. "He's probably not the only one facing depression. I understand the male ego is easily wounded."

They walked into the darkened barn and spent a few minutes talking to their horses. Kelly was stroking her filly's neck when she heard Greg's voice behind her.

"Come here a minute, Kelly."

Glancing around, she saw him silhouetted against the barn door. Walking over to join him, she gasped in delight. Perched on the horizon was a slender sliver of a moon. Its milky whiteness was surrounded by a myriad of twinkling, dancing stars. The air, cleared by the cold front, seemed to sparkle as a gentle breeze stirred her hair. Entranced by the beauty, Kelly stared in silent wonder.

"Kelly?"

"Umm?" Kelly didn't turn around, but her pulse began to quicken as Greg stepped up close and wrapped his arms around her.

"Congratulations on winning the race. I was really proud of you." As Greg spoke, he turned her gently in his arms to face him.

Kelly looked up and met his warm look. He said nothing more. After several seconds he bent his head, and Kelly's pulse began to race. He was going to kiss her! She closed her eyes in anticipation. His kiss was soft and gentle. After just a moment, he lifted his head but continued to hold her close.

Kelly felt light-headed. She had been kissed by boys before, but she had been much younger and hadn't really cared about any of them. Greg was a completely different story. His kiss meant *everything* to her.

"Kelly, I want to tell you something."

Kelly kept her head against his shoulder but nodded for him to continue.

"You're the first girl I've ever kissed."

Her surprise was so great that she leaned back and looked up at him. *The first girl he had ever kissed?* Was he kidding? Surely there had been tons of girls in Texas who wanted to be his girlfriend.

Greg continued in a quiet voice, "Relationships are very important to me. I decided a long time ago that I wanted to honor God in all my relationships —especially the ones with girls. People say kissing and making-out are no big thing, but they are to me. You're special, Kelly. Very special." Leaning down, he gave her one more gentle kiss.

Kelly's voice was barely a whisper. "You're special to me, too." There was so much more she wanted to say, but she couldn't seem to find the right words. They stood quietly for a few minutes, enjoying the night and the sounds of their horses rustling the hay in their stalls.

"I'd better get you home," Greg said at last.

The ride home passed in silence. Kelly knew she didn't want to break the magic of the moment. Evidently, Greg felt the same way.

As she drifted off to sleep that night, Kelly could honestly not remember walking upstairs. She was sure she had floated.

FIVE

Kelly! Hurry up, slowpoke! Greg is here."
Emily's voice drifted up the stairs to the
bathroom where Kelly was frantically getting ready.

"Be right down." Kelly tried to keep her voice
casual. It never ceased to thrill her that she was
Greg's girlfriend, but she didn't want to look silly
about it. Running a brush through her curls and
checking the minimal makeup she wore, she made a
face in the mirror. She'd never win a beauty contest,
but there did seem to be a sparkle to her leftover
from last night's kiss.

Rushing down the stairs, she almost collided with
Greg, who was just sticking his head around the
corner of the stairway to add his call to Emily's.
"Hey, I'm sure it takes time to get looking as great as
you do," he said, "but we're going to be late picking
up Julie and Brent if we don't get going."

"Sorry. We decided to go out for lunch after
church, and the waiters acted like they were robots
in their slow mode. We didn't think we would ever

get out of there. I hope I haven't forgotten anything."

Greg consulted his imaginary Fall Bash checklist. "Bathing suit?"

"Check."

"Blue jeans and sweatshirt?"

"Check."

"Softball glove?"

Kelly turned and dashed up the stairs. "I *knew* I'd forgotten something!"

Seconds later she reappeared in the kitchen where Greg and Emily were laughing together.

"I told you she could forget her head, Greg."

"Um...It's amazing what you find out about people the longer you know them."

Kelly stuck out her tongue and dashed for the kitchen door. "We really don't have all day, *Greg*. Could you please hurry it up?"

Greg rolled his eyes at Emily and untangled himself from the counter stool where he was perched. He lunged after Kelly, catching her just as she reached the passenger door. He pinned her against the side of the car and tickled her until she shrieked for mercy.

"Honestly, you two! The neighbors are going to think we're killing someone over here." Peggy had walked up from where she had been working in the garden and was smiling broadly.

Greg grinned at her. "Have to keep this woman in line, you know. I think all the attention she has been getting has gone to her head. She's forgetting her place of obedience."

Kelly straightened with hastily acquired dignity. "It's a good thing I know you don't mean that, or there could be big trouble. And I bet Peggy would help me take you on."

"Okay, you two, that's enough! Get going, or Julie and Brent will think you're not coming."

Saluting Peggy, Greg and Kelly jumped into the car and eased down the driveway for the ten-minute drive to Julie's house where she and Brent were waiting for them. Nate, the friend Greg had invited to Fall Bash, was meeting them at the church.

"Would you like to pray for Nate before we get to the church? I know he's not a Christian, and I'm really hoping he'll have a good time. His perception of Christians is not real great. I think he's had a few come on pretty strong to him before. He says all they care about is making converts. I want him to see that Christians are real people who just love the Lord."

Kelly gazed with appreciation at Greg. He could be crazy one minute and still think about praying the next. "How about you doing it?" she said. "This praying out loud is still really new to me. I'm not too good at it."

"Practice, Kelly. That's the only way to get comfortable with it. And besides, I'd really like us to be able to pray together about things."

Kelly knew he was right, but that didn't calm the pounding of her heart. She spoke sternly to herself, *Get yourself together, girl. Prayer is talking to God—not trying to impress Greg. Focus on God, then you won't be so nervous.*

She closed her eyes as Greg's deep voice filled the car. "Lord, we just want to pray for Nate today. Thank you he is coming to Fall Bash. Help us to know how to reach out to him. I also pray his heart will be open to the things that are said tonight."

Kelly spoke timidly but from her heart. "Lord, I know that you know all the things Nate is feeling. Help him to let go of any hardness in his heart so he can find you the same way I did."

She opened her eyes to see Greg smiling at her warmly. "You're something else, Kelly Marshall."

The sincerity in his voice enabled Kelly to respond honestly. "You're something else yourself, Greg Adams."

Reaching across the seat, Greg enfolded her hand in his own. They drove the rest of the way in silence, a warm understanding enveloping them.

* * *

The afternoon was full of excitement and fun. A warm front had cruised into the area and made the temperature comfortable for shorts. The competition between the two teams was fierce. Kelly's team, the Conquerors, were ahead of Greg and Nate's team, the Overcomers—up until the last event. The obstacle course Martin had developed proved to be their downfall. The Overcomers overcame Kelly's team with their speed and agility. The competition ended with just six points separating the two teams.

Though the Overcomers boasted only in fun, the Conquerors still yearned for a way to even out the score, even if it was too late for them to win the competition. Martin provided the perfect opportunity.

As the Overcomers paraded around the field, the Conquerors huddled around a huge garbage can that had "miraculously" appeared. Seconds later, they burst forth with a volley of water balloons that turned the boasting into shrieks and yells.

For the next twenty minutes, all-out war broke loose as water balloons sailed through the air on the way to their intended targets. When all the missiles were gone, the whole group dissolved in laughter.

Kelly felt vindicated as she looked at the soaked clothes of the winning team. She had received some hits, but she was fairly dry.

"Hey, Kelly."

Kelly turned toward Greg's voice quickly, eager to show off her dry clothes. Her smile faded, though, as she faced Greg and Nate, both armed with water balloons.

"We don't think you look wet enough," Greg smiled. "We saved these just for you." With that they let loose the huge missiles they carried.

"So much for pride in my dry condition." Kelly laughed good-naturedly.

"Now that you're good and wet, how about a swim?" Kelly stuck out her tongue at Greg, but willingly followed him.

The next thirty minutes resounded with splashes and laughter as Kelly, Nate, and Greg joined the water volleyball in the pool. This time Kelly was on the winning team. Julie and Brent, having lost with her and the Conquerors earlier, groaned that they were meant to be losers.

Julie put on her best pout as they sat together beside the pool after the game. "Only one lousy point, and we would have had you!"

Dinner was a feast of barbecued chicken, corn on the cob, baked beans, hot biscuits, and homemade

ice cream. Dusk was just beginning to color the sky
with its rosy paint when Martin called everyone into
the lodge for the evening meeting. Kelly had stuffed
herself and was more than ready to go relax inside—
until she remembered what lay before her.

Martin had asked her to share what Christ had
done in her life that summer. She was glad for people
to know, but the idea of getting up in front of everyone scared her to death. She had done it at Camp
Sonshine, but it had just been a spur-of-the-moment
thing. She hadn't had long enough to be too scared.
This was different. What if she didn't say the right
thing? What if she messed up?

"Hey, relax. No one is going to throw food, you
know." Greg had correctly interpreted the panicked
look on her face.

"I just don't want to mess up," Kelly wailed.

"Pray about it and ask God to give you the right
words," Greg reassured her. "But hey, God doesn't
care if you mess up. I think he just wants you to be
willing to share. He'll take care of what people think
of it."

Kelly took a deep breath and tried to calm herself. "Yeah, I know all that and it sounds good, but
I'm still scared to death!"

Julie, Nate, Brent, Kelly, and Greg entered the
lodge just in time to snag one of the sofas bordering
the room. Minutes later Martin called the Overcomers to the front.

The Overcomers' cheer filled the room as they
received their awards—frozen candy bars. Kelly
laughed and clapped as they competed with each
other to see who could eat their candy bar then

whistle "Yankee Doodle" the fastest. The contest between Greg and Nate was close, but Greg was laughing so hard that Nate managed to finish the tune seconds before him.

Martin picked up his guitar as the Overcomers returned to their seats. Several group members joined him with their guitars, and for the next twenty minutes songs filled the air. Kelly was glad they weren't all Christian songs. She knew a lot of kids there tonight didn't go to church, and she didn't want them to be turned off. Some of the songs were just fun ones designed to make everyone feel comfortable.

At that thought, the reality of her sharing with the group hit her again—along with the butterflies and doubts. Thankfully, she didn't have long to sweat it out.

Martin put away his guitar and turned to the mike. "We've had a lot of fun today, and we've done some mighty good eating."

He waited for the whistles and cheers to die down.

"Now it's time for a little bit of spiritual food. Fall Bash is a special time for everyone to come together for the new year. It's also a time to find out what God has done in people's lives over the summer. I've asked Kelly Marshall to tell us what happened in her life the past few months."

Martin turned to her with an encouraging smile. "Kelly?"

Greg gave Kelly's shoulder a warm squeeze as she rose to move to the front of the room.

Kelly panicked when she turned around and saw the room full of eyes staring at her. She opened her mouth but nothing came out. Then she saw Greg. His head was bowed, and Kelly knew he was praying for her. Her heart calmed, and she took a deep breath to steady her voice.

"Hi, everyone. I'm Kelly Marshall, and I'm a junior at Kingsport High this year. I've never done this before. I guess I'm pretty nervous."

There was some sympathetic laughter. Several heads nodded their encouragement. Kelly felt herself relaxing.

"I remember going to church some when I was a little kid, but I don't remember much about it, mostly just the cookies and punch I got at break time. Then my mom got cancer and was real sick for several years. We didn't go to church at all. When I was eleven, she died. It was really hard because I loved my mom a lot. I still had my dad, though, and my little sister. We pulled together and became really close. We did a lot of things together but going to church wasn't one of them. It didn't make any difference to me. It had never meant anything to me anyway.

"Well, a little over a year ago, my dad started dating this woman from his real estate office. I liked her at first, but then she and Dad started getting closer and closer. I guess I was pretty jealous because my dad and I had been so close, and suddenly he was spending a lot of time with her. She started coming to our house more and more, and I started to really hate her. Then my dad told me they were going to get married. That was it! I couldn't stand all the change happening in my life. To make it worse, my dad became a Christian and started going to church.

For a while he left me alone about it. After they got married, though, he decided I would have to go to church with them. That made me even madder, and I hated my stepmother even more."

Kelly paused and saw that everyone was listening to her closely. Greg smiled warmly as she continued. "Church wasn't really as bad as I thought, though. The first week I found out about a place called Camp Sonshine that was looking for kids to work with their horse program for the summer. I'm really into horses so that seemed the perfect answer for me. I could do what I loved *and* get away from home at the same time. The only thing was, you had to be a Christian to work there. I wasn't, so I lied on the application and got the job."

Kelly glanced at Nate and noticed an interested look on his face.

"While I was there, I heard a lot about Jesus, but I was pretty good at blocking it out. I don't know that I really had that much against Jesus, but it was just that my stepmother was a Christian, so I had decided I would never be one. I didn't want any more change. Well, it got harder to deal with things, and one day I really blew it. I messed up with one of the classes I was teaching, I yelled at my stepmother on the phone, and then I blew up at Greg. I was just so unhappy. After I did all that, I ran off into the woods where I could be by myself. While I was there crying my eyes out, Jesus made himself real to me. He showed me what an idiot I had been, but he didn't condemn me. All I felt was love. I was so tired of running from everything. I gave my life to him, and for the first time in a long time I had peace about the changes in my life. Since then, I've been trying to grow in Christ, even though I blow it a lot. I'm trying to read my Bible every night, and I'm really trying to become more like Jesus. I have a long way to go, but at least I'm going in the right direction now."

Clapping filled the room as Kelly returned to her seat next to Greg. He reached for her hand as soon as she sat down and whispered, "You did a great job! No one would have even known you were nervous."

"It's just because you were praying for me. Thanks." Kelly snuggled her hand into his and relaxed against the cushions.

Martin took the mike again and turned to the group. "Thanks, Kelly. I have to tell you, though, folks. She left a few things out—like finding her dream horse, and then saving that horse and two others from death during a barn fire that almost killed Kelly. To show their appreciation, the camp gave her the dream horse. I'm sure you'll hear about a beautiful, black filly named Crystal sometime. It seems to be a ready source of conversation for Kelly. She was just too modest to include it in her story."

Kelly blushed and looked down. Several more people came to the front to share their summer experiences, and then Martin took over.

"We've heard some really great stories about what God has done in people's lives," he began. "I know that many of you here tonight are not Christians. You may have heard some things you've never heard before. I hope, though, you heard enough to know that Jesus loves you and wants to be a part of your life. It doesn't matter what you've done. Jesus will forgive you and give you a brand new life. He died on the cross and rose again just so people could have new beginnings."

Kelly watched Nate closely as Martin talked. Her heart ached as she saw the conflicting emotions race across his face. She could tell Nate was struggling with what he had heard tonight. Would he continue to hold out, or would he give Jesus a chance?

Martin smiled at the whole group as he finished. "I want to give you the opportunity to start a new life with Jesus if you want to. If you would like to talk more about it, just come on up here to the front and we'll find a quiet place where we can talk and pray."

Members of the group begin to play their guitars softly. Kelly prayed quietly as she saw several friends from school make their way to the front. Would Nate go up? Kelly watched the struggle go on for several minutes, and then her heart leaped as Nate quietly stood to his feet. Greg grinned and squeezed Kelly's hand before he stood to join his friend. She knew Greg wanted to be able to talk with him and answer any questions he might have.

As the evening meeting came to a close and people began talking and moving around the room, Kelly saw Peggy weaving her way through the crowd toward her. Smiling broadly, her stepmother gave her a warm hug. "I was so proud of you tonight. You did a wonderful job!"

"Thanks, Peggy." Kelly returned the hug but then stepped back quickly. Raging emotions once again tore at her heart. So much of her wanted to accept the love Peggy had to offer, but she just couldn't. What was wrong with her? She could tell

Peggy was aware of the wall she had erected between them. There was a painful uncertainty in Peggy's eyes.

"I'll see you at home," Peggy said quietly. She turned and headed toward the door.

"Okay." Kelly noticed Julie watching her with a curious expression.

"Peggy seems really nice."

"She is."

"What's wrong, then?"

Kelly stared at her friend. "What do you mean?"

"Excuse me if I'm being nosy, but you seem to be really uptight around her."

Kelly heaved a big sigh and looked down. Taking her hand, Julie pulled her toward the porch. "We have some time. Why don't we go outside where it's quiet?"

Kelly nodded and followed her friend out to the large wraparound porch that embraced the lodge. The murmur of the stream muted the noises coming from inside. A soft breeze was rustling leaves that were just beginning to acquire the hues of fall. Kelly gratefully dropped into the rocking chair Julie shoved her direction. Staring out into the night, she lapsed into silence. Several minutes passed.

"Do you want to talk about it?" Julie's voice was gentle and caring.

Kelly fought to stop the emotion that seemed to be always ready to boil over. "I don't really know what to say. I've accepted Peggy, but I just don't know what to do with her. I can't relax around her. I felt like such a hypocrite tonight when I was talking to everyone. Jesus *has* changed my life, but this is still so hard for me."

Julie looked thoughtful. "Knowing Jesus doesn't mean everything in your life becomes perfect and easy overnight. I've been a Christian for three years now, and I still struggle with things. Martin tells me that there will always be times like that. We don't have to expect perfection until we're with Jesus. All he wants us to do is to try, to learn to love him and become more like him."

Kelly nodded. "That's what Greg said, too."

Julie laughed. "Yeah. Great minds think alike. Maybe you should catch the hint."

Kelly laughed, too. "I'm trying." The door to the lodge creaked open and some kids walked out onto the porch. "Thanks for caring, Julie."

"Anytime you need to talk, I'll be happy to listen."

Kelly only nodded.

● ● ●

Anytime you need to talk, I'll be happy to listen.

Julie's words played themselves over in Kelly's mind as she snuggled down on the window seat under a blanket and allowed herself to relive the day.

Her mom had been the last person she had really been able to talk to, Kelly realized sadly. Tears welled in her eyes as she remembered the tender ways her mom used to hold her and talk to her when she was upset about something. Her eleven-year-old problems seemed insignificant now, but the love she had felt coming from her mother at those times was something she desperately missed.

When had she put up her walls? Trying to talk to Julie tonight had made Kelly aware that she didn't know *how* to communicate her thoughts. They were running through her head in wild chaos, but she couldn't force them into words. Kelly sighed. All she could do was hope that eventually her wild thoughts would calm down and she could figure out how to handle all this. That would usually happen if she waited long enough. Usually...

SIX

Kelly joined Greg, Julie, and Brent as they all filed into Sunday school the following week. Martin took just a few minutes to make his announcements and then looked at the class intently.

"I hope all of y'all will listen closely to what I'm going to say. This has been on my heart for a while, and my prayer is that I can share it with you the way I believe God wants me to." Pausing, he picked up his Bible. "How about everyone turning to 1 Corinthians 13."

Pages rustled as everyone found the passage.

"Most of y'all are already familiar with these verses. You probably know it as the 'Love Chapter.' Let me read part of it to you: *Love is patient, love is kind. It does not envy, it does not boast, it is not proud. It is not rude, it is not self-seeking, it is not easily angered, it keeps no record of wrongs. Love does not delight in evil but rejoices with the truth. It always protects, always trusts, always hopes, always perseveres. Love never fails.*

Martin stopped to let the words sink in. Kelly cringed inside. She knew she wasn't doing a great job of loving Peggy, but she really was trying. She had a feeling Sunday school was going to be tough. But Martin's next words caught her off guard.

"You probably think I'm going to talk about loving other people. Well, I'm not. Let me read something else to you. It was written by a teenager friend of mine.

> Accepting love...
> Much harder for me
> Than giving love.
> Insecurities welling up
> Burdening down my heart
> Convincing me down deep
> That no one can really love me.
> So I'm giving and giving
> Yet afraid to open up
> Afraid to accept for myself
> The love others offer.
> When will I be free, Lord?
> To know and experience love;
> The kind you give to all your children
> From you
> And from others around.

Martin stopped again and let everyone think about what he had just read. "You hear a lot about loving people when you become a Christian. And all of that is true. God does call us to love people. He says in Matthew 22:37-39, *Love the Lord your God with all your heart and with all your soul and with all your mind. This is the first and greatest commandment. And the second is like it: Love your neighbor as yourself.*

"Yes, God wants us to love him. And he wants us to love other people. But he also wants us to accept love. That's where I think a lot of us struggle."

Kelly leaned forward to watch Martin closely. Where was he headed with this? she wondered.

He continued, "Y'all are part of a whole generation of kids who don't really know what it means to be loved completely and unconditionally. Maybe your world has been broken by death or divorce. Maybe you have been abused in some way—either physically, sexually, or emotionally. Maybe you are being pressured to be a perfect kid, but you know you can never measure up. Maybe you've made a big mistake somewhere along the way and feel like you can never start over again. Whatever the reason, many of you have put up walls around your heart to protect yourself from more hurt. You want people to love you, but you're not willing to take the risk. It's okay to love other people and give to them, but you don't open yourself to the same thing. Your world is lonely, but at least you feel secure behind your walls."

Kelly listened in amazement. How could Martin know exactly how she was feeling?

"I know letting down the walls is difficult, but I have to tell you that it's the only way to live the abundant life Jesus talks about. Yes, it's scary to open up to someone. Maybe you'll get close, and he or she will leave or let you down. I won't lie to you. That's a chance you'll always take. But Jesus promises never to leave or let you down. And he promises to help you through the hurt times you may experience from other people's actions. And the only way to know real love is to let down the walls. A life lived behind walls is a life controlled by fear, and it will never be the abundant life Jesus promises us. Paul says in 2 Timothy 1:7, *For God did not give us a spirit of timidity*—or fear," Martin explained, "*but a spirit of power, of love and of self-discipline.*

"It is not God who is keeping you behind the walls of your heart. It is Satan trying to rob you of the love and intimacy that God knows you need. Yes, it's important to love, but God knew you could only truly love when you allow yourself to be loved."

Martin smiled gently at the intense faces around him. "I know many of you have been hurt very deeply by circumstances beyond your control. When you're a kid, there's not a lot you can do to change things. But I also know God can heal all the hurt areas of your life. Just bring them to him. He will also put people in your life to help that healing process. But the healing will never happen if you erect walls to keep those people out. Taking down the walls may hurt for a while as you stand face-to-face with your pain, but it's the only way to be free. Your generation is a wounded one, but it doesn't have to stay that way. Jesus can set you free."

Martin stopped and looked around. "I can tell by your faces that I've given you a lot to think about. Know that Janie and I are willing to talk with you any time. I'm praying that all of you will find the courage to tear down your walls and experience the abundant life."

• • •

Kelly was still in a daze when she walked into church and sat down. How could Martin have known her heart so completely? How could he know how much fear she had? She glanced up when Peggy and Emily joined her. Her father would be back tomorrow.

Kelly studied Peggy quietly as the service progressed. She thought of her mother. As music welled around her, Kelly relived the pain of her mom's death—the wasted body that had succumbed to the ravages of the cancer, the months of crying herself to sleep because she felt so alone. It had taken her so long to bring all of her feelings under control. Could she really risk hurting that badly again? Tears choked her throat as Kelly fought to control her emotions. The very effort it took made her decision. The pain was too intense. She just couldn't risk going through it again. She would let people get as close as she felt comfortable with, but no more. The walls would stay in place.

Willing herself to concentrate, Kelly focused on the sermon and shelved the words she had heard in Sunday school that morning. Maybe sometime she could take down the walls, but it wasn't now.

• • •

Excitement shone in Kelly's blue eyes as she and Greg joined the surge of people leaving the sanctuary. Julie and Brent were already standing next to Greg's car when they reached it. Kelly danced the last few feet to join them.

Greg laughed. "Are we just a little excited?"

"I haven't been waterskiing in *so* long! I can hardly wait to try it again. Y'all will probably laugh at me, but I don't care. I just plan to have fun."

Julie tried to look serious. "How can you say we'll laugh at you? Do you think us so cruel?" Encountering Kelly's stare, she started laughing. "Okay. Well, we'll try not to laugh too hard. How's that?"

Kelly tossed her coppery curls in mock disdain. "Do what you want. I won't be able to hear you laugh when I'm behind the boat anyway."

"Or underwater either."

"Huh?" Kelly turned to look at Brent, who was wearing a big grin.

"You won't be able to hear us if you fall a lot and spend most of your time underwater."

Kelly snorted as her friends laughed. "I'm not *that* much of a rookie. I might just surprise all of you!"

Greg stopped laughing and unlocked his car. "Let's change here at the church. I don't want to stay in these long pants one more minute. We sure got our wish for warm weather, but I hear the weatherman said this is our only day of Indian Summer. Tomorrow, fall returns with a vengeance."

Kelly grabbed her stuff and headed for the restrooms. "That's great with me. I'm glad it's warm today, but I'm already in the sweater mode. I'm ready for some more cool weather. So is Crystal."

Julie ran to catch up with her. "I'm with you. I'm thankful for a good day of skiing, but I've had my winter clothes pulled out for a couple of weeks. I'm ready for a change."

A car pulled up alongside Julie and Kelly. Peggy rolled down the driver's side window and smiled at the two girls. "I hope y'all have a good time. Kelly, I forgot to ask you when you'll be home."

"About nine. After we ski we're going to have a cookout on the beach."

"Okay, see you then." Waving, Peggy drove off.

"How have things been going this week?" Julie asked.

"It's been okay. I've been real busy so I haven't been around a lot."

"Isn't your father coming home tonight?"

"Tomorrow. He thought he would be home tonight, but my grandparents asked him to spend an extra day. He hardly ever gets to see them, so he decided to stay."

• • •

Kelly looked around her as the ski boat bobbed gently on the water. It was a gorgeous day. The sky was a brilliant blue with just enough puffy clouds to cast deep shadows on the clear lake. The cove they had driven the boat to was surrounded by tall oaks and maples that were deepening in their fall foliage. Two more weeks and they would be at peak. The cove was smooth as glass but from where she was sitting Kelly could watch scores of sailboats flying across the lake in front of the steady breeze that was blowing. Their colorful sails dotted the water like wildflowers. There were even a few windsurfers who were daring the channel, skimming across the water as they leaned their weight back to counteract the pull of the sail. And, of course, there was a large number of ski boats and the bulkier houseboats full of people out to enjoy the last day of summer weather.

Kelly leaned back and sighed. "I sure am glad you knew about this cove, Julie. I'm too much of a beginner to tackle all the waves the wind and those boats are making. I'd spend all my time underwater for sure!"

Julie laughed. "I'm glad I knew about it, too. Water like that stuff in the channel isn't much fun to ski on even when you're good. You spend all your time fighting the waves and the wakes and end up exhausted."

"It's a miracle this cove is empty," Brent added. "It's like having our own private ski area. Smooth water is always the most fun."

"All this discussion is great," Greg said, "but let's hit the water! Who's going first?"

Julie spoke up. "Why don't we let Kelly go? I need to show Brent the specifics of driving this boat before he pulls me. He's driven lots before, but every boat is different."

Greg reached for the life jacket Kelly was going to wear. "Time to suit up." Walking over, he held the jacket while Kelly slipped her arms through. Then he steadied her on the small platform on the back of the boat until she dove in. "One ski, or two?"

"Very funny! If you want me to do anything other than sit in the water, you'd better send me both. Come to think of it, maybe three would be helpful."

"You'll have to settle for two." Greg lifted the fiberglass skis and then deftly pushed them across the water to her.

Kelly had only skied a couple of times, and that had been several years ago, so she paid close attention as Greg gave her instructions.

"Bring your knees up to your chest like you're trying to sit on your skis. Make sure the tips stay out of the water. Keep the rope between the skis and just let the boat pull you out of the water. Make sure your arms are straight and your knees bent just a little." Greg paused and then grinned. "Oh, and if you fall, make sure you let go of the rope. It's hard to breathe when you're doing a face plant in the water at high speed. I've seen people actually forget to let go of the rope."

Kelly stuck her tongue out at him and then concentrated on remembering everything he had told her. Julie circled the boat to bring the ski rope around to her and then gradually pulled out the slack.

Looking back, Julie shouted, "I'm going to drag you for just a little bit to give you a feel for your skis. When you're ready, yell, and I'll bring you up."

Kelly nodded and allowed her body to adjust to balancing over the skis as Julie gently drug her through the water. It took only a few seconds to get comfortable.

"Ready!"

"Here we go!" With those words, Julie pushed down hard on the throttle.

Kelly was concentrating so hard on Greg's instructions that she didn't even realize she was standing until she heard her friends cheering. A wide grin split her face as she skimmed across the water. Once she felt secure of her balance, she dared to glance around. She took in the beauty of the afternoon and enjoyed the feel of the water and wind washing her body.

Dimly she heard Greg yelling something to her. Watching him carefully, she saw him waving her to go outside the wake of the boat. Kelly hesitated. She had never before tried to venture over the wake. The crests of water looked like mountains as they spewed out behind the boat. But why not? she thought. This was a day for new things. Leaning her body a little to the right, she felt the skis respond. Leaning more, she moved to the right and onto the wake. Once she started over it, however, she hesitated. So instead of both skis skimming across to the safety of the smooth water on the other side, one ski stayed behind. She was straddling the wake. Trying to bring her skis back together to move out caused her to lose her balance, and she fell backwards into the water.

Grabbing the skis, Kelly lay back and waited for the boat to circle around to her.

"Way to go. You got up your first time!" Greg congratulated her.

"It was really fun. I didn't do such a great job crossing the wake, though. I've never tried that before."

"Want to try it again?" Julie offered.

"Of course I do. I'm not going to let a mountain of water stop me."

Greg grinned. "That a girl. Go for it. You'll do it next time."

It took Kelly a few more attempts before she could cross the wake without falling, but she finally conquered it. By then her arms were shaking with the strain, and she was ready for a break. Releasing the ski rope, she allowed herself to sink gently into the water and then climbed into the boat as it came around.

Julie smiled at Kelly's exuberant expression and then waved Greg toward the back of the boat. "You're next, Greg."

Greg proved to be quite an expert on two skis. Kelly watched in admiration as he skimmed across the water, tackling the wakes with ease as he moved back and forth behind the boat. After about ten minutes, Julie eased back on the throttle and settled him into the water. Once he had let go of the rope, she brought the boat back to where he was waiting.

He looked disappointed. "Is my time up already? It feels like I just got started."

Brent grinned down at Greg. "I'd say it's time you tried your hand at a slalom ski. You're great on two, but one is much more fun."

Greg grinned back. "Hey, if y'all have the patience to wait it out while I try, I'll be happy to. I've always wanted to learn to ski on one ski."

Greg listened carefully as Brent told him what to do. "Balance is the key when you're trying to get up on one. Some people like to start out on two, drop one off, and keep going, but I think that's harder. I always lost my balance. Once you get the hang of coming up on one, it's easy. Your strong foot goes in the back of the ski. I always put the rope on the right side of my ski. You'll have to see what works best for you. The biggest difference is the strain on your arms as the boat pulls you up. You'll want to let go, but just hang on. Concentrate on keeping your ski straight and your body centered over it. Then just let the boat do the work. This is a powerful boat, so that makes it a lot easier."

"Okay, let's give it a try!"

It took Greg four times before he was able to come up, but once he was up he adjusted quickly to the difference. He whooped and called from behind the boat as he experimented with his new-found freedom.

When the boat pulled around to pick him up, he spoke excitedly, "Boy, you're right! What a difference! I felt like I could fly. I'll never ski on two again."

Kelly tossed him his towel as he climbed into the boat. "You looked great out there. I'm impressed."

Greg laughed as he bowed low. "You should be impressed! You didn't think I would fail when I was showing off for you, did you?" Wrapping the towel around his waist he pulled her down onto the seat beside him. "It's time to watch the pros now. I think we're in for quite a show."

He was right. Brent and Julie had both been skiing for years and seemed intent on outdoing the other. Kelly watched with delight as they flew across the water, jumped the wake, and created huge rooster tails by digging deep into their turns. Brent was definitely the more powerful of the two, but Julie had an ease and gracefulness that made her skiing beautiful. Kelly was content to settle back into the arm Greg had thrown around her and watch. The sun felt wonderful on her body. She felt every part of her relaxing. Home and Peggy seemed far away.

It was about five when they finally pulled up to the dock. Each of them had had an opportunity to ski again. By the time they had finished putting the gear into the boathouse, they were tired and starving. Brent emerged from the boathouse with the large cooler Julie's parents had left for them.

"Here's dinner!"

Julie smiled. "You found it. Great! Let's see what they left for us. Probably hamburgers." Opening the lid, she yelped, "Steaks! They left us steaks. Boy, they know how to make the last day of skiing special." Rummaging through the cooler she continued her inventory, "There's baked potatoes already wrapped in foil, some salad, and a loaf of French bread also wrapped in foil. We can heat everything on the grill. And what's this? All right! A chocolate cake. My mom makes the greatest chocolate cake in the world. Wait till you taste it."

The rest of the group was impressed. "I'm feeling spoiled," Greg said. "Your parents are something else."

"Yeah. They must really like you guys. Most of my other friends just get hamburgers." Julie grinned and then spoke to Brent. "How about if you guys get the gas grill going and move the picnic table down under the tree next to the beach? Kelly and I will set everything out, and then you guys can cook the steaks."

"Your wish is my command—especially when you're paying me with steak!" Brent laughed.

Everyone worked quickly, and it wasn't long before they were digging into the incredible meal. Silence reigned as they satisfied their hunger. When the last morsel of chocolate cake had been devoured, they leaned back from the table, content to soak up the peace of the late afternoon. The sun was dipping low on the horizon, casting a golden glow over the world. Kelly was entranced by the golden sparkles dancing on the water as the waves and ripples caught the waning light.

Julie was the first to speak. "It's only seven. We have time for one more ride. What do you think? The lake is almost empty. I can show you where they are building the new power plant on the lake. It's pretty cool to look at."

The other three exchanged glances and nodded. Kelly spoke up eagerly, "Sounds great to me! If this is our last day of warm weather for a while, we might as well make the most of it. It only takes thirty minutes to get home, so we have plenty of time."

Greg agreed. "Let's do it!"

After a quick cleanup, they were once more skimming across the water. The late afternoon stillness had turned the channel into a huge mirror. There were only a few other boats out to mar the surface. Kelly felt like they were in their own little world as they sliced through the water.

It took about twenty minutes to reach the site where they were constructing the power plant. The place was a beehive of activity.

"They're working twenty-four hours a day to get it done, so there is always something going on. At night it's really cool to come watch all the lights reflecting off the water." Julie throttled the boat to a standstill.

After a few minutes, Julie headed the boat into a cove branching off to the left.

"This cove is my other favorite place to ski," she said. "There are some beautiful homes down here. Hardly anybody lives here year-round, though. They mostly just come for weekends. It's pretty deserted by Sunday evening. I think y'all will like it."

After taking them all for a tour of the cove, Julie turned the boat back toward the main channel. "It will be dark in about thirty minutes. If I push it, we'll be back in fifteen minutes and just make it home." No sooner had the words left her mouth than the boat coughed and glided to a stop.

A few seconds of confusion passed and then Julie slapped her hand against her forehead. "I can't believe I was so stupid! We're out of gas. We're stuck in this deserted cove, and we're out of gas!"

SEVEN

The four looked at each other in concern. It was going to be dark soon, and there was no way to call for help. Silence fell on the group as they contemplated their situation.

Greg was the first to speak. "Well, we can't just sit here. We've got to at least *try* to get help. Didn't I see some old paddles stashed on one side of the boat?"

"Yes. My dad put them there for emergencies. But Greg, we're talking four or five miles. It will take us all night to paddle across the channel. And we don't have any lights. What if another boat hits us?" Julie's voice was tense.

"But Greg is right," Brent spoke up. "We have to do *something*. We can't just sit here. No one will think to look back here, and we sure won't have people just cruising by in this cove. Maybe we should just try and paddle to the main channel. Didn't I see a flashlight on the boat somewhere? We could flash the light to make sure no one hits us. We can also use it as a signal."

Julie groaned and covered her face. "I'm so sorry!

This is all my fault. If I had just paid more attention, I would have known we were running out of gas. All I could think about was having some more fun."

Kelly moved over to comfort her friend. "Hey, don't worry about it. We'll figure something out. And in the meantime, this is a great adventure. What a story we'll have to tell at school tomorrow. Besides, all of us are due home in an hour. When we don't show up, someone will come looking for us. It'll work out."

"Kelly's right," Greg added. "It's not like we're going to starve out here or something. We're still stuffed from dinner. We're not in the middle of a big storm. We're just floating around. We might as well have fun!"

Julie laughed reluctantly. "Okay, you guys." Reaching down next to her, she pulled out two paddles. "Who wants to go first?"

Greg and Brent reached for the paddles in unison. "You and Kelly keep a watch out for boats," Brent said. "We'll paddle. It shouldn't take us too long to make the main channel. Maybe thirty minutes. When we give out, if we do in such a short time, we'll switch."

Kelly and Julie scanned the shoreline again as the boys took their positions on either side of the boat. If someone would come home to one of the houses, they could paddle in and phone for help. But all of the grand houses remained shrouded in darkness. They had no choice but to head for open water.

• • •

Greg was the first to stand erect and flex his aching muscles. Brent followed suit. The look they shared was one of concern.

Kelly spoke their thoughts. "We're not getting very far are we?" They had made progress in the last thirty minutes, but they were still deep in the wooded cove.

"Nope," Greg responded with frustration. "I think the cold front they predicted is coming through. We're paddling straight into the wind. We're moving, but we're not going anywhere fast."

Kelly nodded as she wrapped her arms around herself for warmth. The temperature was definitely dropping. The shorts and shirt which had been so adequate for the warm day were woefully inadequate for the cutting wind that was beginning to blow.

Julie stood to take the paddle from Brent. "Kelly and I may not make headway as fast as you and Greg, but you can't paddle all night. Besides, it will help us get warm. It's your turn to look out for boats."

Brent nodded and handed her the paddle. The group was quiet as the girls struggled to move the boat forward against the increasing wind. It was only twenty minutes before their muscles were screaming in rebellion. Reluctantly they handed the paddles back to the boys who dug in with renewed energy.

Greg grinned at Kelly. "Thanks for the break. If y'all can help out on short stretches like that, it will be great."

Kelly looked down at her watch and groaned, "It's already nine, and we're only halfway out of the cove! What are our parents going to think?"

Brent added his concern to hers. "Yeah, my mom will probably freak out. She's gotten so protective ever since Dad left."

Kelly looked at him sympathetically. Brent's father had left his mother for another woman. Unbidden, Martin's words earlier that day rose in her mind. *Y'all are part of a whole generation of kids who don't really know what it means to be loved completely and unconditionally. Maybe your world has been broken by death or divorce. Maybe you have been abused in some way—either physically, sexually, or emotionally. . . . Whatever the reason, many of you have put up walls around your heart to protect yourself from more hurt.* Kelly wondered if Brent had any walls around his heart. If he did, he hid them really well. But then, so did she.

The four of them said nothing while the boys paddled the boat forward. It took another hour, and the girls giving the boys two more breaks, before they broke out into the main water of the channel. One look convinced them they would never be able to paddle across the expanse of water stretching before them. The wind fighting them back in the cove had been difficult, but the buffeting they were enduring now would be impossible to overcome. Whitecaps rolled around them as the boat bobbed and danced in the water. The four friends looked at each other in renewed concern.

"What do we do now?" Kelly's voice had lost its edge of adventure and betrayed the cold and fear she was feeling.

Greg moved over to wrap his arm around her. Grateful, she leaned into the warmth of his body as he spoke. "I'm not sure. But there's one thing I know we should have done a whole lot earlier. We need to pray. For two hours we've been fighting this on our own."

The rest of the group nodded in agreement and bowed their heads while Greg prayed. "Lord, we're sorry we didn't come to you sooner about this. We've gotten ourselves into a mess and need your help. I ask you to show us what the best thing is to do. And please help our parents not to worry too much. Amen."

"Amen." The chorus of the other three fled before the blowing wind. They sat in silence for a few minutes until Julie spoke.

"Since we can't fight this wind, maybe we should just let the wind blow us back down the cove. At least we could find a boathouse or something where we could be warm and wait for tomorrow."

Brent shook his head in disagreement. "We've made it this far. I think we should keep trying to get help. My mom will be a complete basket case if I don't show up all night. She'll have me dead and in a morgue somewhere. I know how her mind works. I don't want to do that to her."

"I agree with Brent," Greg said. "I've also been thinking. The power plant isn't too far down the lake. That's why it's so light out here. That place is lit up like a Christmas tree! The wind is blowing in that direction. How about if we paddle down to the construction site? I bet we can get help there."

The three contemplated his words and then all nodded.

Kelly smiled at him. "I think that's a good idea. Let's try it."

The boys picked up the paddles and renewed their efforts. Kelly leaned back and tried to regain her sense of adventure. In spite of the cold, it was a beautiful night. The blowing wind had polished the sky to a brilliant ebony. There were so many stars they seemed to merge. Even the Milky Way was evident as it streamed across the sky.

"It's beautiful, isn't it?"

Kelly nodded her head silently in response to Julie's quiet voice.

"It's hard to not believe in God when you see something like this," Julie continued softly. "How could anyone think this was a big mistake or the result of an explosion in the sky? Only a God who loves us would have gone to this much trouble to create such beauty."

Again, Kelly just nodded in agreement. She was beginning to enjoy herself once more. If God could handle creating all this, then surely he could handle the problem of a little boat bobbing on cresting water. Gradually, she felt herself relaxing.

Greg's shout startled her out of her reverie. "All right! There it is. I knew we could make it. Now we just have to paddle the boat over to shore and go in for help." His triumphant voice quickly changed to one of dismay. "Good grief!" he exclaimed. "Look at all those rocks. If we take the boat near those things, we'll be goners."

The other three clustered at the front of the boat and looked where he was pointing. For hundreds of yards in both directions, huge rocks and boulders lined the beach and the slope rising up to where the power plant was being built. Help was within their reach, but it might as well have been a hundred miles away. The wind was blowing them in the direction of the dam, and rocks lined the beach all the way to it. They would never be able to turn around and fight the wind back to where the beach was clear.

Silently, they considered what to do.

Suddenly Greg rose and began to peel off his shirt. Kelly was alarmed. "What in the world are you doing?"

Greg's voice was determined. "We need help, and we're not going to get it this way. We can't bob around out here all night. It's too cold. And besides, we might not be able to keep the boat away from the rocks. I'm not keen on explaining to Julie's parents why their boat is at the bottom of the lake. I'm going to swim ashore and get some help."

"I'm coming with you." Brent rose to take his shirt off as well.

"I don't think that's a good idea," Greg said. "You need to stay and help keep the boat away from the rocks. It won't take me long to swim to shore. I'll be back with help as soon as I can."

Brent nodded reluctantly. "We'll do our best to keep the boat in the same general location. If the power plant has a boat handy, they'll probably come tow us in. If not, they'll call the Lake Patrol and have them come help us."

"Right." Greg poised on the side of the boat for a few moments, flashed a grin at Kelly, and dove into the inky water. Thankfully, there was enough light from the power plant for them to watch as his sure strokes sliced the water and propelled him toward the rocks. Minutes later they saw him pull himself up onto the rocks carefully. He clambered to the top and then turned to give a wave as he disappeared over the crest.

Once he was out of sight, Julie, Kelly, and Brent went to work. The current and the waves kept driving the boat toward the rocks, so they rotated turns as they paddled just enough to keep the boat bobbing in its same general position. Kelly prayed as she paddled and wondered how Greg was doing. In spite of her concern, she was heartened by the fact that help was surely headed their way soon.

• • •

Greg climbed over the mountain of rocks and made his way down to the single lane paved road running through the complex. He had entered the power plant at an area where nothing was happening that night. Sitting down, he untied his shoes from the belt loop where he had fastened them. He had known better than to try and swim with soggy, heavy tennis shoes on his feet. It had been no trouble dragging them in the water behind him as he swam, though. He had almost left them in the boat, but now he was glad he had them to hike through the complex. Turning to the right, he headed toward the lights and commotion. He had gone only a few hundred yards when he heard the whine of a motor behind him. Grateful to have found help so quickly, he turned toward the lights speeding up on him. As the vehicle skidded to a stop, Greg began to walk toward it. He halted abruptly as two men jumped from the jeep, one of them holding a pistol.

"Hold it right there, kid," the man with the gun said.

"What's going on?" Greg asked in confusion.

"We could ask you the same thing. This whole area is off-limits to the public. What do you think you're up to?" The tall, burly guard spoke with a rough, menacing tone.

Greg hastened to explain. "Our boat ran out of gas a couple of hours ago. We managed to paddle out of the cove we were in, but there was no way we were going to make it across the channel. There's four of us. The other three are still in the boat, and it's getting really cold out there. We weren't sure we could keep the boat from crashing into the rocks, so I swam to shore to find help."

"Sounds like you have a pretty active imagination, son."

"It's true! Climb the rocks and you can see for yourself. There's a boat out there with two girls and a guy in it." Greg was concerned but not really afraid. He knew he was telling the truth, and when they figured that out, they would surely help him.

The burly guard who had spoken looked skeptical. The other guard, a smaller guy who Greg guessed to be in his twenties, spoke up. "He could be telling the truth. This isn't exactly a great night to be out for a casual swim, Sam. And he wasn't exactly trying to hide his presence here."

Sam mumbled something under his breath but turned toward the jeep and grabbed the radio. "This is Security calling the tower," he said. "Come in, please."

The receiver he was holding crackled to life. "Go ahead, Sam. We read you."

"I've got a kid down here with some wild story about a boat with three kids in it that's run out of gas. He claims he swam to shore to get help."

"Hold on. I'll look."

The radio went silent for several seconds while Greg and the two guards quietly inspected each other. Greg decided the burly guard didn't really look that menacing. His rough face had a kind quality, and his eyes were mild as he watched Greg.

The radio crackled back to life. "I've got them in sight. There's three of them in the boat. Two girls and a guy. Two of them are paddling. Looks like they're trying to hold the boat in its same spot. I'll call the boat slip and then get back to you."

"Roger. We're going to take this kid..." Releasing the button he gazed at Greg with a friendlier expression. "What's your name, kid?"

"Greg. Greg Adams."

"Right." He spoke into the radio again. "We're going to take Greg over to the security hut and give him something dry to put on."

Greg grinned gratefully. The shaking of his body was about to become uncontrollable. Dry clothes sounded great. He needed no urging to clamber into the back of the jeep behind the two guards. Soon they were ushering him into the warmth of the small trailer serving as the security hut. Greg quickly threw on the thick coveralls they tossed to him. The radio crackled to life as he was zipping them up.

"Okay, Sam. Jim's going to drive the boat. He's filling up a five-gallon can with gas now. Bring the kid down and he can ride out to meet them. Jim's going to get the boat going and then escort them across the channel."

Relief flooded Greg's body.

"Looks like everything is going to be okay," Sam said to Greg. "Let's go."

Greg turned to follow the two guards and then stopped. "Hey, could I use the phone for a minute? I'd like to call my folks and let them know I'm okay."

Sam nodded and pointed to the phone. It took just a few minutes for Greg to assure his parents they were all fine and to ask them to call the other parents to fill them in. "It's eleven now, Mom. By the time we get back to Julie's boathouse and get home, it will probably be about twelve-thirty. Thanks for understanding."

Hanging up the phone, Greg made one last request. "Since your guy is going to follow us back, could I have three more coveralls for my friends? I bet they're freezing by now. We can give them back when we get to my friend's boathouse."

Coveralls in hand, Greg jumped in the jeep for the short ride to the boat ramp. The pilot was already in the boat waiting for them. Greg turned to shake the hands of the two guards. "Thanks for all your help. You scared me pretty good at first, you know."

Sam laughed. "Yeah, well that's our job. We get all types around here."

Greg nodded and then settled down in his seat as the boat roared to life. In minutes the boat soared across the whitecaps to where Julie's boat bobbed helplessly in the water.

Kelly's voice was the first to greet him. "You made it! I don't think I've ever seen anything that looked as good as your boat flying across the water toward us!"

Julie's voice broke in, "Did you have any trouble?"

Greg grinned. "Oh, other than being apprehended by two security guards with a pistol, there was no problem. I'll tell you the whole story later."

"Man, am I glad to see you," Brent said. "I wasn't sure how much longer we could keep the boat off the rocks. The wind is blowing harder, and we were losing the battle."

Greg nodded. "Meet our lifesaver Jim. He's got gasoline, and he's going to follow us back over to the boathouse to make sure we get there all right. Oh, and I almost forgot!" Reaching back down into the power plant boat now securely snugged against Julie's, he pulled out the coveralls.

"Warmth!" Kelly yelped with joy as she reached over to grab the pair he offered her. "My body thanks you!" She pulled on the bulky outfit and then snuggled down into a seat to watch Greg and Brent help Jim with the heavy gas can. It was only a few minutes before the comforting roar of Julie's engine filled the night.

"Hurray!" The four of them cheered in unison as Jim jumped back into his boat and unlashed the ropes holding them together.

"I'll follow you guys. You shouldn't have any trouble, but I'd rather play it safe."

Greg smiled. "We appreciate all your help." The other three nodded vigorously as Julie throttled the boat toward home.

Now that they were safe and warm, the ride turned into a fun adventure. They all laughed as Greg recounted his swim and his initial concern when Sam approached him with a pistol. After a few minutes, Greg pulled Kelly to the back of the boat. Sitting down on the floor where there was less wind, he motioned Kelly to join him. With his arm around her, they sat back with their heads on the seat, watching the stars glowing above.

"All's well that ends well," Kelly murmured.

"Umm." Something in Greg's voice caused her to turn her head.

She closed her eyes just as his mouth came down on hers in a gentle kiss. When he moved away and she opened her eyes, Kelly was sure the stars were spinning. Greg smiled and then pulled her head down on his shoulder. Closing her eyes again, Kelly allowed the wonder of the night to fill her soul. What could be better than being snuggled next to Greg in a boat flying across the water, pursued by millions of stars that knew the secret of their kiss?

• • •

Kelly could barely keep her eyes open on the drive home. All she wanted to do was walk in the house, climb the stairs, and fall into her bed. Getting up for school tomorrow was going to be torture. Greg dropped her off first. She was not surprised to see lights on in the kitchen. Kelly was sure Peggy would be as ready to go to bed as her. Pushing the door open, she stepped into the warm comfort of the kitchen.

Peggy was sitting at the kitchen table, sipping on a cup of coffee. "Kelly," Peggy said with obvious relief, "you gave me quite a scare."

Kelly smiled tiredly. "It was quite an adventure. I'll tell you and Dad all about it tomorrow after school."

"I'd like to hear about it now. How did this happen?"

Kelly halted her advance to the stairway and looked at Peggy quizzically. There was a hard edge to Peggy's voice she had never heard before. Was she mad?

"Julie's boat ran out of gas, and we got stranded on the lake," Kelly said slowly. "I thought Greg's parents called and told you."

"I know the boat ran out of gas. But why? It seems to me Julie was being pretty careless."

Kelly's body stiffened at the tone of Peggy's accusation. "It was a mistake. She felt bad about letting it happen."

"She should have," Peggy remarked stiffly.

Kelly felt her irritation rising. "Look, it was an accident. Besides, everything turned out okay. We're fine."

"Yes, everything turned out okay, but it seems like y'all didn't stop to think very much. You never should have gone back out on the lake that late. Didn't you know there wouldn't be any other boats around if you needed help?"

The magic of the night evaporated. "I don't know why you're making such a big deal about it," Kelly threw the words in anger. "We handled it just fine. The boat is fine. We're fine. Everything is fine!"

Peggy's voice reflected the same anger. "Yes, and there are four sets of parents who have been sitting up worried out of their minds. Brent's mother was especially upset. Did you ever stop to think about that?"

Kelly's anger exploded. "Yes, *Peggy*, I did stop to think about that. That's why Greg called from the power plant. I don't know what else we could have done. And there were only *three* sets of parents worrying about their kids. My father is gone, and there was only a stepmother who doesn't know how to mind her own business *here!*"

As soon as the words escaped Kelly's mouth, she was sorry. The stricken look on Peggy's face only made it worse. Bursting into tears, Kelly turned and fled up the stairs.

EIGHT

Kelly felt like she was drugged as she reached over to turn off the alarm. She lay there for a moment until a noise downstairs in the kitchen brought back to life last night's battle with Peggy. Kelly was sure her eyes were puffy and swollen from all the tears she had shed crying herself to sleep. Remorse flooded her as she relived the ugly scene. She still felt like Peggy had been unfair, but that didn't excuse the things she had said. What would her father say? And what must God be thinking of her right now? She had been so sure becoming a Christian would take care of all the problems with Peggy. What was wrong? Maybe she just wasn't cut out to be a Christian.

Swinging her legs over the bed, Kelly sat up and stared out her window. She knew she had to get moving, but her tired body just didn't want to function. Hearing a noise, she turned her head toward the door. Peggy stood framed by the morning sun streaming in the hallway window.

"May I come in?" Peggy asked quietly.

Kelly nodded and turned her body to face her stepmother. She figured Peggy was going to let her have it.

"I came up to apologize for the way I acted last night." Peggy's words took Kelly completely by surprise. She could only stare as Peggy continued. "I was worried, and I took it out on you. I'm sorry I came across wrong and made you angry. Will you please forgive me?"

Kelly only nodded. She knew she needed to apologize as well, but she couldn't force the words to come out of her mouth.

Peggy stood gazing at her for a few moments and then smiled gently. "Bowls of cereal are out on the counter. I have to go into the office early today to check on a house contract for your father. He's flying in around noon and will pick you up at the stables."

Kelly cringed inside at her words. She had missed her father terribly and wanted to see him, but she could just imagine what he would say about her latest fiasco.

"Have a good day at school. And try to stay awake." Peggy smiled again and then walked from the room.

Kelly stared at the empty doorway for several minutes. Now she *really* felt bad. How could Peggy come in and apologize like that? She had seemed to mean it, and she hadn't said one word about the horrible things Kelly had said to her last night.

Emily stuck her head in the door, and her eyes widened when she saw Kelly still in her pajamas. "Kelly! The bus comes in fifteen minutes. You'd better hurry. I thought you told me you had an algebra quiz this morning."

Kelly groaned and forced the problems with Peggy out of her mind. Jumping up, she ran into the bathroom. She had forgotten all about the algebra quiz. She had planned on studying for it last night when she got home from skiing. Skipping a shower, she settled for washing her face and pulling her hair back into a ponytail. She hastily put on a pair of jeans and slipped on a red shirt to match the red band she had secured her hair with. Making a face at her reflection, she ran down to the kitchen. She wasn't hungry, but she knew she needed to eat.

She had gulped down the last bite of cereal when she heard the bus round the corner. Grabbing her books, she sprinted after Emily and clambered on the bus just as the driver was closing the doors.

• • •

The rest of the morning didn't go much better. She didn't do very well on her algebra quiz. Not only had she not gotten to study, but her tired brain seemed unable to concentrate on the problems. Fortunately, at least, her grades up to this point had been good. One small test wouldn't do *too* much damage.

French went just as badly. Hatchet-face Grimsley seemed intent on picking on her, and Kelly's tired brain just refused to function. She couldn't distinguish between male and female nouns, no matter how hard she tried. Grimsley apparently found joy in humiliating her, but Kelly was heartened by the sympathetic looks she was getting from fellow students. Many of them had heard the story about her late-night adventure and knew she was exhausted.

Her friend Corrie leaned over near the end of class and whispered, "Don't let her get to you. She must have gotten up on the wrong side of the bed *and* drank bitter lemonade this morning. Isn't she a joy?"

Kelly smiled in spite of herself. This day would end sometime. In the meantime, she only had ten more minutes of Grimsley and then Greg would be meeting her for lunch. At the thought of Greg, her mind flooded with memories of the night before— the fun, the fear, the cold, the special kiss they had shared under the stars. She hardly noticed the rest of French class. The clanging bell jolted her from her thoughts. Picking up her books, she moved toward the door where she knew Greg was waiting.

"Kelly, I hope you'll do us the favor of having both your body *and* your mind in class tomorrow." Mrs. Grimsley's words were direct.

"Yes, ma'am." Kelly mumbled as she ducked out the door. Greg waited for her with a sympathetic grin.

"I already got the word from Corrie. Sounds like Grimsley already had lunch today. You."

Kelly laughed up at his handsome face. "Yeah. I hope it gives her indigestion!"

Greg laughed with her, reached down for her hand, and started down the hall. The day was *definitely* improving. They had walked arm-and-arm down sections of the hallway before, but this was the first time he had held her hand. Kelly thrilled at the envious looks thrown her way.

"How was Peggy last night when you got home?" Greg's words jarred her from her happy thoughts.

"My parents had been worried, but they were cool once I explained it."

Kelly didn't want to talk about her problems with Peggy. It made her feel too much of a failure. She forced herself to respond lightly, "Oh, she was fine. I was beat last night when I got home, so we went straight to bed." Kelly cringed at adding lies to her swiftly growing list of sins, but she just didn't know how to communicate the confusion and hurt she was feeling.

Greg regarded her closely for a minute, but finally nodded. "That's good. I was hoping there wouldn't be any problems. I wasn't sure how it would be without your dad there."

Kelly was saved from having to say anything else by Brent and Julie walking up to join them for lunch. Greg asked them how their parents had reacted. Both said that their folks were worried but had understood the situation—and they appreciated Greg calling his mom and dad from the power plant.

It took them a few minutes to get their food. Kelly wasn't hungry for the salad she had built, but she had a long afternoon at the stable before her. Granddaddy had asked her to help with a new horse that was coming in. It wouldn't do to be both tired *and* hungry.

As they sat down at their usual table, Greg and Brent quickly got involved in a conversation over the current standing of the soccer team. Kelly concentrated on her salad and tried to stay awake.

"Have you gotten your dress for the Homecoming Dance yet?"

"No." Kelly turned to converse with Julie. "My dad has been out of town. We decided to have a special night and pick it out together. He's going to take me out to eat and then we're going shopping. It'll be sometime this week."

"Your dad is going to go shopping with you?" Julie asked in surprise. "My dad wouldn't be caught dead shopping with me for a dress. I'm sure he would go insane if he tried to do it."

Kelly laughed. "My dad and I like to shop together. He had to go with me after my mom died. Besides that, he has good taste. It's fun sometimes to get the male perspective on what I'm buying. I do most of my shopping on my own now, but he offered. I'm looking forward to it."

Julie nodded. "I'm jealous. It does sound like fun. Just a little strange."

They excitedly began discussing dress colors and styles. Hearing the conversation, Greg turned his attention away from Brent.

"So where do you lovely ladies want to go for dinner?" he said. "Brent and I thought it would be fun to turn the evening into a foursome."

Kelly and Julie exchanged looks of delight as Kelly replied, "Why don't you guys choose the place and surprise us?"

Greg and Brent both smiled and nodded. "You got it, my girl," Greg said. "Nary a word will pass mine and Brent's lips until the big night. You will just have to wonder."

● ● ●

"What's this horse like, Granddaddy?" Kelly stood watching as the truck and trailer wound its way up from the road.

"I don't know. At least I'm not sure. A friend of mine called and said he had some neighbors who wanted to get rid of their horse. They have plenty of money, so they didn't want anything for him—they just wanted him to have a good home. I might be making a mistake taking him, but my friend seemed to think this horse was worth the trouble and time to work out his problems. We'll see." Granddaddy stopped talking as the rig rumbled to a halt. "I'll tell you more about him once we get him settled in."

Kelly nodded and moved over to assist in opening the back door and lowering the ramp.

"Here you are, Mr. Porter. He's all yours. Where would you like him to go?" The slightly built man who stepped from the truck looked to be in his mid-thirties and had thinning blond hair. He reached over to help Kelly with the latch on the gate.

"Let's just get him out of there," Granddaddy replied. "I'm going to let Kelly take charge once we get him off. She knows where I want him to go."

I'm going to let Kelly take charge. Granddaddy's words thrilled her. It was obvious he had confidence in her. All her hard work was paying off. Stepping back, she watched the driver unhook the rump chain and then allow the big gelding to back off. Taking stock, Kelly was impressed with the build and muscle of the chestnut quarter horse. He was tall and sturdy with alert eyes and a well-formed head. He looked to be no more than three or four. Stepping forward, she took the lead rope the driver offered her.

"Watch your step with him, miss," the driver cautioned. "You never know what he's going to do."

Kelly looked at him quizzically. "What's his problem? Is he mean?"

The driver squinted as he gazed at the gelding. "Well, no. I wouldn't say he's mean. *Spoiled* would be a better word for this one, I guess." Latching the gates back on the trailer, he turned to Granddaddy Porter. "Good luck. I've got to pick up another horse."

Granddaddy nodded. "Thanks for delivering him." Waving goodbye to the man, he turned to where Kelly stood waiting.

"What's his name, Granddaddy?"

"Jason."

"Jason? What kind of name is that for a horse?"

Granddaddy smiled. "The people who raised him named him after their oldest son who was killed in a riding accident. The son's mare had just had Jason a couple of months before that, only then his name was Buddy. Anyway, their son was riding the mare when something spooked her and she went down. It was a freak accident. The boy fell off, broke his neck, and died instantly. The mare broke her leg in three places, so they had her put down. They just couldn't bring themselves to get rid of the colt."

"The driver said to watch out for him. What's the problem?"

Before Granddaddy could answer, the gelding began to bob his head and paw the ground impatiently. Kelly tightened her grip on the rope, but he just pulled at his head harder.

Granddaddy began to walk toward the barn. "Let's go ahead and put him in the paddock. He needs to move around some. I'll finish his story then."

Kelly nodded and led the impatient gelding in the direction Granddaddy was headed. He calmed down once he was moving, but Kelly was aware of the watchful way he was eyeing her. It made her a little uneasy. She didn't take her eyes off of him. Just as she was putting out her hand to open the paddock gate, Jason's head snaked out with bared teeth. Snatching her hand back just in time, Kelly used her other hand to smack him on the nose. Hard.

"Good move, Kelly. That's just what Jason needs. Seems he thinks he can get away with anything he wants. He's got some lessons to learn."

Kelly was shaken at her close call but grateful for Granddaddy's words. Holding Jason's head more firmly, she unlatched the gate, let him walk through, and then unhooked his lead rope. As soon as he was free, the big gelding trotted over to the other side of the arena to call to the horses out in the pasture.

Granddaddy leaned back against the gate and finished Jason's story. "The driver hit it right on the head, I think. Jason is a very spoiled young gelding. Like I said, after the owner's son died, they decided to keep the colt. But it seems it was the son who knew a lot about horses; his folks knew next to nothing. They basically treated him like a pet—like a dog, I suppose. Until he was ten months old, they allowed him to come in on cold nights and sleep on the rug beside the fire."

"What?" Kelly's voice registered her astonishment.

"Yeah. I agree it's not exactly the preferred method of teaching a horse to be a horse. The people did him no favors. He's three-and-a-half, and the only thing he knows is how to wear a halter and be led around. And as you know, he doesn't do that too well. When he started nipping as a colt, they thought it was cute and didn't discipline him. Now it's turned into a full-scale biting problem. That's why they finally decided to get rid of him. Two weeks ago he latched onto their ten-year-old daughter's arm. She had to have twelve stitches."

Granddaddy sighed. "Any farrier trying to trim his feet has the devil's time of it," he continued. "They've run through the last farrier in the area who will come out. One farrier had the right idea, though. When Jason started doing his thing, the farrier tied his feet and pulled him down on his side. The owners were horrified he would do that. But that's probably the best lesson this spoiled brat has gotten in his whole life. Unfortunately, the owners quit using that farrier."

Granddaddy stopped talking a moment to study the well-built animal trotting around the paddock. "He's got tremendous potential, but it's going to take a lot of work. He thinks he's a pet and that no one has the right to demand anything of him. If you ask him to do something he doesn't want to do, he becomes mean and looks for a way to get back. Pouting might be cute behavior in some dogs, but in a two thousand pound horse it can be downright dangerous. I'm hoping that some good discipline will convince him that human beings are something to be respected. He'll be much happier."

Kelly looked again at the animal. "Why did you take him, Granddaddy? Surely he could never be a class horse. You wouldn't be able to trust him."

"You're right. But there are always people looking for a good horse, and Jason's a fine animal. I
have a hunch that with some strong discipline and a
lot of tough love, Jason here will make someone
a terrific horse. You know, Kelly," Granddaddy
looked at her softly, "you can't be afraid to deal with
a problem. The only way to solve it is to face it—and
get help, if you need to."

Kelly could feel tears forming in her eyes. Granddaddy always seemed to know when something was
bothering her. But she said nothing.

Granddaddy reached for the lead rope Kelly had
placed on the fence. "He looks like he's calmed
down some. How about taking him inside to groom
him? Keep a close eye on him. If he tries to bite you,
let him have it on the nose. Hard, like you just did.
He'll eventually learn the efforts aren't worth the
discipline."

Kelly nodded. "Thanks for trusting me with him,
Granddaddy."

"You've earned my trust. If you want to be a horse
trainer someday, you need to learn how to deal with
all kinds."

By the time Kelly had groomed Jason, she was
exhausted and ready for some time with Crystal. He
had tried to bite her ten times in the first five minutes. Only careful watchfulness had saved her from
being part of his next meal. Her hand ached from
swatting him on the nose. During the remaining
thirty minutes he had eyed her watchfully, but had
only attempted to bite four more times. Kelly knew
that retraining this dangerous gelding would take
time, but she was excited by the challenge. She was

also very thankful for the loving, easygoing temperament of her own beautiful filly.

• • •

Kelly allowed Crystal to meander slowly through the leafy woods. Crystal's alert ears and springy step indicated an eagerness to go, but the ebony filly seemed to sense Kelly's fatigue and so was willing to walk along. Kelly was well aware of Crystal's mood, but she was just too exhausted to respond. The adventures of the night, the fight with Peggy, the pressures of school today, and the challenge of Jason had drained her of all energy. She wanted to do nothing more than ramble along and drink in the beauty of the day.

The same cold front that had been so frightening on the water the night before had blown in beautiful, crisp weather for the afternoon. Kelly was grateful for the thick sweatshirt she had put on before leaving the barn.

As Kelly rode, a heaviness settled in her heart. She thought about God, but didn't feel she could talk to him. She had really blown it with Peggy the night before, but it was so much more than that. There seemed to be a large vise around her heart that wouldn't let go. No matter how hard she tried, she couldn't free herself from its grip. Not even being with her beloved filly lightened the heaviness that was suffocating her. Kelly rode until her watch told her it was time to put Crystal away before her father came. That thought did nothing to make her feel better. What in the world was he going to say about last night? With a sigh, Kelly turned back toward the barn.

•   •   •

"How's my girl?"

Kelly heard her father's voice and felt his arms envelop her in a hug. She had been leaning over Crystal's stall, stroking her neck. Now she spun around to return her father's hug. "Dad! Welcome home."

"It's good to be back. I missed you."

"I missed you, too. How was your trip?"

"The trip was fine. Standard real estate business stuff. The time with your Gramps and Gram was good. They send their love."

Kelly nodded.

Her father hesitated before continuing. "I hear you had quite an adventure last night."

Now it was Kelly's turn to hesitate. How much had Peggy told him? He seemed pretty relaxed. Surely she couldn't have told him about their fight yet. Maybe she had decided to give him a good homecoming and save the heavy stuff for later.

Her father noticed her hesitation. "I also hear the ending of your night was kind of rough."

Kelly flushed and looked at the ground. He knew.

"You want to talk about it?"

Kelly continued to stare at the ground in silence.

"What's the problem, Kelly?" her dad asked gently. "Things seemed to be so much better, but now you've put up some kind of huge wall. I'm concerned about you, honey."

Kelly felt tears choking her at the kindness in his voice. Why didn't he just yell at her? She could have handled that. But this! She could feel her control slipping, and she fought to maintain it. How could she explain what she didn't understand herself? She knew she had to say *something*, though.

"I'm sorry about last night. I guess I was just really tired." Her voice was tight from the struggle to keep control of her emotions.

Her father pressed harder. "It's more than that. I'd like to be able to help, but I can't if we don't talk about it. I know we haven't done a lot of deep talking up to this point, but I think I've always been here for you."

Kelly looked up quickly. "You've been great, Dad. It's not that I don't want to talk to you. It's just that I don't know what to say. I don't know what's wrong." Her voice faded off miserably, and her gaze returned to the ground.

"Okay, hon. I want you to know I'm willing and ready to talk if you want to. In the meantime, I think you owe Peggy an apology. She told me she thought she handled things poorly last night, but I think there's blame on both sides."

Kelly nodded silently.

Her father regarded her quietly for a few more moments and then turned toward the barn door. "Let's go. Peggy probably has dinner waiting. And I have a feeling you're going to be ready to hit the sack early tonight. Are you as tired as you look?"

Again, Kelly nodded.

On the drive home Kelly looked at her dad thoughtfully. She may be struggling with the whole concept of being a Christian and loving other people, but her dad had changed into a new person. The old Scott Marshall would have let her have it. He would have gotten angry and then apologized and hugged her. She thought maybe she preferred that. At least she could get defensive, and then they could make up. This new way put all the pressure on her because it was impossible to fight with his kindness.

Delicious aromas of chili and cornbread assaulted Kelly's senses as her father opened the door to the kitchen, but she wasn't hungry. The heaviness of her heart and the tiredness of her body had stolen her appetite.

She watched silently as her father gave Peggy a hug and a kiss. Taking a deep breath, she spoke as Peggy turned to greet her.

"I want to apologize for the things I said last night. I didn't really mean them. I was tired and didn't handle things well. I'm sorry." Kelly knew her voice was tight, but her effort would have to do.

Peggy began to move toward her, but seeing Kelly stiffen, she halted and merely smiled gently. "Thank you, Kelly. I forgive you. Both of us were tired last night."

Kelly nodded. "Do you mind if I don't join you for dinner? I'm not hungry. All I want to do is take a shower and fall in bed. It's been a long day."

"That's fine," Peggy said softly. "I know you must be beat. I'll put a plate in your room in case you feel like eating after your shower."

Kelly smiled gratefully and headed for the stairs. As she passed her father, he reached out and gave her hand a warm squeeze.

Thirty minutes later she lay snuggled under the comforter on her bed. She had left her window open to enjoy the cool breeze flowing in. She glanced at the Bible on her nightstand but was both too tired and too despondent to pick it up. The heaviness had not diminished under the pulsating warmth of the shower.

NINE

Kelly was pretty sure hatchet-face Grimsley had discovered that today, as had been the case yesterday, Kelly's body was in French class but her mind was somewhere else. She was doing her best to concentrate, but it was impossible. How could she care about French verbs and sentence structure when her heart felt like a cinder block? Sleep had done nothing to improve her frame of mind. What was *wrong* with her? Rising from her seat at the end of class, she felt Julie's eyes on her.

"Are you okay, Kelly? You've seemed to be somewhere else all day."

Kelly nodded wearily but tried to infuse a positive note in her voice. "I'm fine. I think I'm still just tired from the other night." She knew her friend was concerned, but talking wouldn't help. She just wanted to be left alone to sort out her feelings. Until then, she would have to do a better job of hiding her true emotions. Forcing a smile, she continued, "My dad and I are going shopping tonight for my homecoming dress. Have you gotten yours yet?"

Julie nodded excitedly. Kelly's attempt to distract her was successful. "I got it last night. I'll tell you all about it at lunch. Brent has a doctor's appointment today, so he won't be eating with us. I don't mind Greg hearing about it, but I want to surprise Brent. Speaking of Greg, there he is now."

Kelly turned as Greg walked into the room. Taking a deep breath, she summoned all of her control and stuffed down the feelings of confusion and pain threatening to overwhelm her. "Hi, Greg!"

"Hi, yourself. Hello, Julie. You two ready for some lunch?"

Kelly slipped her arm in his and smiled up at him. "You bet! I'm starving."

Greg returned her smile but looked at her face closely. Kelly could see the question in his eyes, but he didn't say anything. *Good grief!* Kelly thought. *Was he able to read her mind?* Kelly realized she was going to have to try harder to be cheerful, so she chattered all the way down the hall. She talked about homecoming, about Jason and how he had tried to bite her, about her frustrations with French. She was relieved when they reached the dining hall.

"Excuse me a minute. I need to go to the restroom," Julie said abruptly and headed off in the opposite direction.

"What's wrong, Kelly?" Greg's quiet question caused Kelly's heart to sink. Her efforts weren't working.

"I don't know what you're talking about. I'm fine, just hungry and maybe still a little tired from the other night." She forced a grin.

He merely shook his head. "If you don't want to talk about it, that's fine. But I know something is wrong. Your face is smiling, but your eyes tell me something else. You ought to know by now I can tell if something's wrong."

Kelly cringed inside at his words. All she could do was stare at him.

"I'm willing to listen, if you decide you want to talk about it."

Kelly struggled to fight down the emotions welling within her. She didn't want to cry! Knowing she was losing the battle, she choked out, "I'm sorry, Greg," and turning, she fled. She didn't know where she was going. She just knew she needed to be alone. She needed time to think, time to gain control.

Without being aware of how she got there, Kelly found herself in the woods behind the school. She stood still under the canopy of trees and took deep breaths until she felt control returning. What in the world must Greg be thinking? She just needed a few minutes. Then she could go back in and apologize and make up some reason for her emotional condition. She supposed she could always blame it on the time of the month. Sometimes being a female was a benefit.

"Greg said he thought you would come out here."

A soft voice behind Kelly caused her to whirl around. "Julie!"

"Greg said you got pretty upset and took off. He's really concerned about you, Kelly. So am I. What's wrong? You haven't been yourself at all for the last few weeks. It's like you're playing some big game. You don't want any of us to know something is wrong, but it's not working."

Kelly's heart sank within her. How could her feelings be so obvious? For so long she had been so good at hiding them. Why not now? All she could do was stare at the ground.

"We're your friends, Kelly. We want to help. Is it Peggy? I know that's been hard for you."

The sincere caring in Julie's voice encouraged Kelly to at least attempt to share some of her thoughts. "It's not Peggy," she began hesitantly. "Well, maybe it is. Oh, I don't know! Things are just so confusing right now." Julie was quiet as Kelly struggled with her words. "It's not that Peggy is doing anything. She's always nice to me—*really* nice. I guess it's just that she's there. I'm just not used to it."

"Tell me about your real mother," Julie said gently.

"My real mother?" Kelly's voice reflected confusion. "Why do you want to know about my real mother?"

Julie shrugged. "I don't know." She pressed on. "Were you close?"

Kelly allowed a small smile. "Yeah. My mom was the greatest. She would do anything in the world for me." She paused for a moment. "Every night she would come up to my room, and we would talk. I couldn't go to sleep until I had told her about my day."

"It must have been really tough for you when she died."

Kelly could only nod. No one knew how much she had died inside when her mom had succumbed to the cancer. She had not shared her true feelings with anyone. She was used to handling things on her own.

"You must have been pretty angry when she died."

"What?" Kelly stared at her friend. "What in the world do you mean?"

Julie looked uncertain but pressed forward. "My aunt died two years ago. It didn't affect me that much because we weren't really close, but my cousin went through a rough time. She cried a lot at first, and then she got angry. She was mad because her mom wasn't going to be there for her anymore. Even though she knew her mom was sick and couldn't help dying, she felt deserted. Then she felt bad because she was angry. It took her a long time to deal with it."

Kelly could not stop the tears from welling up in her eyes. Miserable, she stared at the ground and fought for control.

"Have you ever talked to anybody about your mom's death, Kelly?"

"No." Kelly's voice was small, but she knew she needed to say something. "Look, I'm sorry, but I'm not used to talking about this."

Julie nodded. "I can tell. But you're not too good at playing games anymore either. You may think you're hiding everything, but the people who really care about you can tell. Did you ever think God might be wanting to help you deal with this by using your friends?"

Kelly shrugged, again not knowing what to say.

"Look, Kelly. You won't ever feel any better about this if you keep hiding behind your walls. You think the walls will keep anymore hurt away from you. Actually, all they do is keep out the love others want to give you. Walls can make you pretty lonely."

Kelly was listening—really listening—but she had no words to respond.

Julie changed tactics. Her questioning became more direct. "Are you afraid to let Peggy get close to you? Is that why you stay so angry with her? So that you don't have to deal with your feelings and maybe get hurt again?"

Kelly's thoughts whirled around her. Confusion, pain, and fatigue all threatened to overwhelm her. "Julie, please! I don't know what I'm feeling. I don't know what to think. Give me some time!"

Kelly saw a hurt look flash across Julie's face, but her friend gave a small smile. "Yeah. I hear you. Look. Just know you have friends who care about you and who want to help you when you want it." Turning away, she threw over her shoulder, "Class starts in fifteen minutes. Greg said he would wait outside the main entrance for you."

Kelly stared after her. The churning was worse, but Julie definitely had given her a lot to think about. Kelly hoped she hadn't hurt her friend, but she just couldn't find the words right now to express what was going on.

• • •

Kelly was silent as she and Greg wound through the woods on Shandy and Crystal. He had given her a big hug when she had met him at the school's main entrance after lunch, but he hadn't questioned her. She was grateful to him for giving her space. She wanted to talk to him, but she just couldn't yet. He seemed to be content to ride along beside her and be lost in his own thoughts.

Kelly had been thinking all day about what Julie had said earlier. Her friend's question about being angry at her mom had stunned her. How had Julie been able to know that? Kelly had never admitted it to another soul. She tried not to admit it to herself. How in the world could she feel anger? Kelly wondered. But she did. And it made her feel incredibly guilty. It wasn't her mother's fault she had died. But then, it hadn't been hers either. And she was the one who had been left to struggle through life without a mom.

Kelly could feel tears swelling her throat and was relieved that the foursome was approaching the pasture. She knew she needed to give Crystal a good run today. Her filly had been extremely patient with her quietness yesterday, but Kelly could feel the eagerness building in Crystal.

Swallowing hard, Kelly forced a smile and took a deep breath. "I think these two would appreciate a run. What do you think? Do we give it to them?"

Greg's answer was to loosen the reins and lean forward as Shandy broke free of the woods. The big buckskin tossed his head and surged forward. All Kelly had to do was allow a little slack to enter her reins. Crystal leaped forward as if being released from prison. Neck and neck they raced across the pasture to the big oak. No one made an attempt to declare a winner. Kelly was content just to be flying alongside Greg and Shandy. She knew Crystal was happy as well.

After reaching the oak, Greg and Kelly circled the horses and angled toward the woods on the far side. Crystal and Shandy may have wanted to run, but they didn't need to run at breakneck speed the entire time. Pulling them down to a fast canter,

Kelly and Greg exchanged smiles and concentrated on enjoying the fun.

Kelly never ceased to be amazed at the smoothness of her filly's gaits. Even at a fast canter, Kelly felt as if she were just floating along. She had ridden other horses where she had to work hard to stay secure in the saddle, but with Crystal she didn't even have to think about it. It was as if they were one—in body *and* mind. After thirty minutes of cruising around the field, Kelly felt much more positive about life. The rushing wind and the glorious sun had blown away the cobwebs and infused her with life once more. Her problems were still there, but they would work out. She had always been able to gain control of her emotions before, and this was no exception. Kelly was filled with relief. Emotions and feelings were fine, she thought, as long as she stayed in control of them.

• • •

"Hey, Dad. What do you think of this one?" Kelly held up a red dress for her father's inspection.

Her father eyed it carefully and then shook his head. "I like the blue one better."

"But everything I've bought lately is blue. Greg must be getting sick of it."

"I hardly think so. Blue is your color. Especially that shade. It makes your eyes come alive and goes so well with your tan. I can't imagine Greg could get tired of seeing you at your best. Judging by the way he looks at you, though, you could probably wear anything and he wouldn't care."

Kelly blushed. "Oh, Dad!"

Her father laughed. "Well, it's true! If he wasn't such a great young man, I would be extremely jealous. As it is, I guess I just have to keep an eye on him. And maybe you *should* choose the red dress. The blue dress might look *too* good."

Kelly laughed at his good-natured teasing but put the red dress back on the rack and headed to the dressing room with the blue one. The evening with her father was proving to be great fun. He had picked her up from the barn, given her time to take a quick shower to wash off horse smells, and taken her to her favorite restaurant for dinner. Nothing had been said about Peggy, and Kelly had felt herself relax. The afternoon ride on Crystal had done much to restore her equilibrium. She was beginning to feel like herself again.

Glancing in the mirror, Kelly knew her father had been right. His wolf whistle as she walked out to show him his choice wiped away any remaining traces of doubt.

"Poor Greg," Dad commented. "I almost feel sorry for the boy. Women aren't supposed to look this good!"

Kelly reddened but laughed in delight. She could hardly wait for next week and the Homecoming Dance.

• • •

Two hours later Kelly was curled up in her favorite post—the window seat guarded by her leafy oak sentinel. Gone were the shorts and T-shirts of the summer. Pulling her fluffy robe tight around her body, she was grateful for the warmth it provided against the chilly wind blowing in the open window. Soon it would be too cold to leave the window open. She planned to enjoy these crisp fall evenings for as long as she could.

A light tap sounded at her door. Maybe her father had come up to tell her once again how wonderful their evening had been.

"Come in." Kelly was taken aback when Peggy moved into the room and gently shut the door behind her.

Nothing was said for a couple of minutes as Peggy came and gazed out the window with her. Finally her stepmother spoke, "I understand why you like this spot so much. It's peaceful."

Kelly nodded and waited to hear the reason for Peggy's visit.

"Kelly, I know I apologized yesterday, but I still feel like I need to talk to you." Pausing, she looked at the window seat. "Do you mind if I sit down?"

Silently, Kelly moved over to make room.

"I was worried Sunday night when you didn't come home, and I was tired, too," Peggy began after she settled in. "But there was more to the reason I handled things so poorly. I felt like I needed to tell you. This being a stepmother is scary business. I've never had kids of my own, and now suddenly I have two—and two who had a very wonderful mother of their own for a long time. Then you managed just fine with your father for five years, and now suddenly you're supposed to accept a new person in the house. I can imagine how hard that must be. Kelly, I don't want to replace your mother. I know I could never do that. I just want to be your friend. I'm going to mess up a lot, I'm afraid, as I try to figure out how to act, how to handle this new role I find myself in. Mostly I just want you to know I care very deeply for you and am trying very hard to understand where you are coming from..."

Peggy's voice trailed off. Kelly sat very still and felt her heart yearning to be close to this woman who cared enough to be honest. She and her mother had had these type of honest talks. How Kelly longed to unburden herself on Peggy, to release the pain eating at her core. She opened her mouth, but nothing came out. She was sure the confusion she was feeling was evident on her face.

Peggy waited a few more moments and then rose. "Thanks for listening, Kelly. I'll see you in the morning."

All thoughts of sleep fled as Kelly stared after Peggy's retreating back. So much of her screamed to call Peggy back, but she said nothing. The walls around her heart seemed to be impenetrable. Tears flowed freely as she stared into the inky blackness of the night. The conversation she had had with Julie earlier that day invaded the fake peace she had so carefully put together that afternoon.

Are you afraid to let Peggy get close to you? Is that why you stay so angry with her? So that you don't have to deal with your feelings and maybe get hurt again?...

You think the walls will keep anymore hurt away from you. Actually, all they do is keep out the love others want to give you. Walls can make you pretty lonely...

But you're not too good at playing games anymore either. You may think you're hiding everything, but the

*people who really care about you can tell. Did you ever
think God might be wanting to help you deal with this by
using your friends? ...*

You must have been pretty angry when she died...

Words and feelings collided in Kelly's head as she
fought to regain control. Finally, she slipped down
on her knees. For too long she had been fighting this
battle on her own.

"Lord, I'm afraid of what's going on inside of
me," Kelly prayed. "I don't know how to handle all
the things I'm feeling. I used to be able to block out
the pain, but I can't do that anymore. Maybe Julie is
right. Maybe you are trying to help me deal with the
pain. Maybe you are trying to use my friends to help
do that. But God, I just don't know what to do. I
don't know how to talk about what's going on inside
of me. If you want me to, you're going to have to
help. I don't know how to bring down the walls."

Tears continued to rain down on her pillow until
Kelly fell into a deep slumber.

TEN

"**K**elly Marshall! You're going to wear that mirror out by staring into it. I already told you, you look great!" Emily pranced into her room and flopped down on her bed. "It's just a date. You don't usually go ga-ga like this."

Kelly sniffed indignantly. "I'm not going *ga-ga*. But this happens to be a *very* important date. It's Homecoming, and it's my first dance. And Greg has made reservations at a really nice restaurant..."

"You've told me this a hundred times!" Emily interrupted. "I know you're going to some wonderful surprise restaurant. I know Greg worked millions of hours for his dad to earn the money. I know this is like the most *wonderful* restaurant in the country." Pausing, she grinned. "Am I leaving anything out?"

Kelly glared at her, then turned to look back in the mirror. "Do I really look okay?" She knew the new blue dress she was wearing was flattering. It was strapless, the first one she had ever owned, and it fit her snugly at the waist and then flared out into soft folds down to her calves. Her dad had given her a big whistle when he saw her in it, but that didn't really count. He was her *father*. Dads are supposed to make their daughters feel good about how they looked. He had even surprised her with beautiful earrings and a matching necklace—gold surrounding blue stones the same color as her dress. She twirled once in front of the mirror to catch the effect.

"You don't look okay. I keep telling you, you look great!"

Peggy breezed into the room. Emily turned to her for reinforcement. "Peggy, she's driving me crazy. All she does is stare into the mirror and ask me if she looks okay. I hope I don't act this ga-ga when I have a boyfriend."

"I keep telling you, I'm not acting *ga-ga*—whatever that stupid word means, anyway. It's just that this is important." Kelly's voice rose to a high pitch.

Peggy laughed. "Okay, you two. Cease fire. Emily, I predict that in the near future, you will enter the ga-ga phase yourself. Kelly, come here." Peggy took her hands and then held her back and viewed her critically. "Take it from an old woman who knows. You'll have Greg eating out of your hand tonight. You look sensational!"

Kelly blushed, but smiled. "Thanks, Peggy."

Emily snorted. "Oh sure. Believe *her*. She says one word, and you say thanks. I told you the same thing, you know!"

Just then the doorbell rang. Kelly swooped down and gave her startled sister a kiss on the top of her head. "Thanks, Em. I guess you were right after all." Whirling from the room, she heard Emily give the last word.

"Ga-ga. Absolutely ga-ga!"

Greg's admiration was obvious as Kelly rounded the corner to the kitchen where he was talking to her father. He had only one word: "Wow." Then he just kind of stared at her.

Scott Marshall laughed. "It's not really fair for women to do this to men, you know. They look like that and knock you off your feet, don't they?"

Greg just nodded.

Peggy must have been right. Kelly thrilled at the feeling which swept over her. It was so fun to look and feel special. She wouldn't like to dress up all the time—she would always be more comfortable in jeans and sweaters—but every now and again was all right.

"You look really great tonight," Kelly said shyly. And he did. His mother had insisted on buying a new suit for him. She had said it was a good excuse to make him go shopping for something besides jeans and sweatshirts. His suit was a soft gray with tiny white pinstripes. A light blue shirt adorned by a colorful tie made him look pretty incredible. Kelly felt lightheaded at the thought of the evening ahead of them.

Greg's eyes spoke volumes, but his voice was casual as he took her hand. "Brent is waiting in the car. We have to pick up Julie. We better get going."

It took only a few minutes to reach Julie's house. Greg and Kelly waited in the car while Brent went to the door to get her. Greg turned and took Kelly's hands in his.

"Happy Homecoming, Kelly. I'm glad we're going out tonight."

"So am I. Happy Homecoming to you, too."

They just looked at each other. Kelly felt silly, but it also felt okay to be looking at him without saying anything. Seconds later, the car door opened and Julie and Brent slipped in.

Brent's deep voice filled the car. "Now that we're all here, and looking pretty spectacular, I might add, let's get going!"

Kelly and Julie exchanged looks of delight as Greg bowed low from his post behind the wheel and pulled out of the driveway. Kelly peered out of the windshield, hoping to guess their destination before they arrived. She exchanged glances with Julie when Greg turned the car down Amherst Boulevard. There was only one nice restaurant in this part of town, but surely the boys weren't taking them *there*.

Conversation centered around their football team's victory over arch-rival Clinton High in the homecoming game the night before. Kelly was glad the dance was the night after. It made the evening more special and the homecoming weekend longer.

Both girls drew in their breath when Greg slowed to turn up the long drive. They *were* going to The Drawbridge. Greg caught Kelly's look of delight. Reaching back over the seat, he exchanged a solemn handshake with Brent.

"I think our attempt to please our dates has been successful." Greg grinned.

"*The Drawbridge*," Julie said in awe. "I've always wanted to come here. Wait till our friends hear. They'll be green with envy!"

Kelly was equally pleased. "I wouldn't have guessed in a million years. My dad says it's the finest restaurant in Kingsport."

The restaurant sat high on a hill, one side overlooking the twinkling lights of Kingsport's small business district and the other the frothing water of the river rapids. Parking in a lot near the bottom of the hill, they walked up a steep path of natural stone lit by lanterns and then over a heavy timbered drawbridge to enter the restaurant's reception area. The entire place was built of rough hewn stone and was lighted exclusively by lanterns and flickering candles. The host had led them down a dark corridor that opened into a high-ceilinged room crowded with flourishing plants and small tables spaced well apart. Their table sat next to a beveled glass window overlooking the river. Lights, placed discreetly in the shrubbery, illuminated the rapids in the darkness. Kelly was glad they were getting the view of the river. She was sure Greg had asked for it. Their table was a stone slab, and the chairs were crafted out of rough wood lashed together with leather strips. The soft velvet padding was the only concession to luxury. An ornate lantern attached to the wall provided their only lighting. Peggy had told her dim lighting always enhanced someone's best features. Kelly hoped she was right.

"Like it?"

Kelly turned to Greg with excitement shining in her eyes. "I love it. I never imagined anything like this!"

"This is absolutely wonderful," Julie echoed Kelly's enthusiasm.

The boys exchanged subtle high-fives. Kelly was touched to know that what she and Julie thought meant so much to them.

The dinner passed with much laughter and talk.
The food was excellent, and Greg even talked Kelly
into trying a raw oyster. She ate it but was repulsed
by the feel of the slimy thing sliding down her throat.
She managed a smile but refused the next one he
offered. She was quite happy with the shrimp cock-
tail she had ordered as an appetizer. She had almost
refused to order one once she saw the prices, but
Greg had seen her face, interpreted it correctly, and
told her to get whatever she wanted. He had plenty
of money. Kelly couldn't help but feel special.

Everyone was stuffed by the time they had finished dessert. The boys paid the bill, and, laughing,
they lumbered back down the stone steps they had
skipped up two hours earlier.

"How in the world are we going to dance now?"
Kelly rolled her eyes.

Greg laughed. "Once you hear the music, I'm
sure you'll come back to life. You'll have to! I love to
dance, and I refuse to have a chair potato on my
hands."

His words were soon proven true. As soon as
Kelly entered the noise and excitement of the gym,
her energy and high spirits returned. In a moment
they became a part of the moving, laughing mass
crowding the dance floor.

Kelly was amazed at how comfortable she felt
dancing with Greg. She had never done much dancing, but she found her body moving naturally to the
beat of the music. She was surprised to find how
much she enjoyed it. Things really kicked into high
gear when the band started to play music for a line
dance. Kelly had heard of line dancing, but she had

never tried it. It took her a few minutes to get the hang of the steps, but once she did, she and Greg blended in with everyone else stepping and dancing across the floor. She even saw several of the teachers and some of the parents join in the fun. She was laughing and out-of-breath by the time the music stopped.

Gasping, she begged for a break. "I've got to have a drink, Greg."

"You got it. Wait right here." Greg and Brent blended into the crowd and then disappeared from sight.

Kelly turned to Julie. "I never knew you could have so much fun at a dance. Just think of what I've been missing."

Julie laughed but couldn't resist teasing her. "Are you sure it's the dancing you're enjoying so much—or Greg? He can't keep his eyes off you, you know. He's so smitten I almost feel sorry for the boy."

Kelly blushed but laughed. "I must confess it's mutual. Isn't he something else? But I don't think he's the only guy who's smitten tonight. I think Brent suffers from the same condition. Wasn't it incredible of them to take us to The Drawbridge? It must have cost them a fortune."

"I'm sure it did," Julie agreed. "Of course, it was pretty easy for Brent. His dad is loaded so he just gave him the money. That's how he tries to make up for walking out on them for another woman. But Greg had to work like crazy for his dad to earn it. Smitten—definitely smitten!"

The boys returned with their drinks, and Kelly drank hers gratefully. As she handed Greg her empty cup, the band broke into a soft, slow song. Tossing their cups into a nearby trash can, Greg turned and took her in his arms. The fast dancing and the line dancing had been fun, but slow dancing had them beat hands down. Kelly allowed him to pull her close, and then she closed her eyes and allowed the music and the feelings to wash over her.

• • •

Greg pulled into Kelly's driveway and turned the car off. Turning, he took her in his arms. "I had a great time tonight."

"I had a great time, too. Thanks, Greg. Thanks for everything."

She rested there for a few minutes and waited for the kiss she was sure would come. They didn't kiss very much, but she always loved it. She was surprised when Greg straightened up instead.

"Kelly, can I talk to you about something?"

She could tell by his voice he was uncomfortable. "Sure. What is it?"

"Well, I've been doing a lot of thinking lately." He hesitated, and then blurted out, "Kelly, I really like you a lot."

Kelly waited. This was no revelation. Something else was on his mind.

"I've been thinking a lot about what Martin talked about last week at youth group," he finally said. "About how hard it is to stay pure sexually when you're a teenager. About how dangerous it is to start being physical with your boyfriend or girlfriend because sometimes you start something you can't stop. About how many relationships are messed up by sex and being too physical."

Kelly blushed bright red and was glad the car was dark. She knew Greg was fighting to express himself, so she simply reached out and took his hand.

He took a deep breath and continued, "Kelly, I don't ever want our relationship to get messed up. And sometimes, when I kiss you, I start thinking things I know I shouldn't be thinking. Not that I ever want to do anything," he hastened to reassure her. "I don't ever want to hurt you. But I don't even want to think like that. I want God to be able to bless our relationship, not feel bad about it." He stopped. "Do you know what I'm trying to say?"

Kelly spoke slowly. "I think so. I heard the same thing, you know. That night I was thinking about it and decided I want to stay a virgin until I get married. I had never really thought a lot about it before—at least not until I met you. I know a lot of kids at school who are already having sex, but I want to keep that to give as a gift to my husband."

Greg nodded. "I feel the same way. I just wanted you to know why I don't kiss you very much. I think it's okay to do it sometimes, but I want to be really careful. It would be easy to get carried away. You're just so pretty!"

Kelly blushed furiously again and didn't know what to say. She had certainly never had this kind of conversation with a boy before. But she *had* been thinking about it, and she was glad they had talked. No further words were necessary, though. Greg took her in his arms again, and they were content to sit in silence.

ELEVEN

Kelly yawned and stretched as she waited for Mandy to join her in the chilly, early-morning sunlight. Last night had been wonderful, but four hours of sleep were going to make for a very long day today. It had been worth it, though. She smiled as she thought of all the things she and Greg had talked about. She was grateful, too, that he hadn't brought up the issue of Peggy. He seemed to know she would talk about it when she was ready.

"Good morning, Kelly."

"Hi, Mandy. Good thing you've got your jacket. It's cold this morning!"

Nodding in agreement, Mandy stopped long enough to shove her arms into the sleeves of her thickly lined denim jacket. "Fall is here to stay, I think. I love these cold, crisp mornings followed by cool days. There is no better weather for working with horses."

"That's for sure!" Kelly smiled. "Granddaddy said something about working with Jason this morning. What are we going to do?"

"Our little brat needs some work on tying. We made the mistake of assuming he knew how to tie the other day. It took me two hours yesterday to put the fence pole back in the ground and to fix the slats he broke."

Kelly whistled. "Jason is three years old, and he doesn't know how to tie?"

"Nope. Seems his owners tried it when he was young. He didn't like it, so they never did it again. They just let him do his own thing when he felt like it. Now we've got a two thousand pound spoiled brat on our hands."

"What are we going to do?"

"First, we need to see if he won't tie because of fear or stubbornness. If it's fear, then we'll take it nice and easy. Granddaddy thought it would help to tie Crystal next to Jason. That way he can figure out that if Crystal isn't scared of it, he doesn't need to be either. It will take some time, but it will eventually work. If it's stubbornness, then we need to teach him a lesson about respecting humans—before he or someone else gets hurt."

Kelly nodded in agreement. "Do you want me to go get Crystal or Jason first?"

"You go get Crystal and tie her to the third fence post. I'll go get Jason. I'll bring him out and tie him to the tying post. That way if he goes nuts, he won't be near enough to hurt your filly."

Kelly disappeared into the barn and appeared moments later with Crystal. As she tied the filly to the post, she handed over the carrot Crystal was nosing her pockets for. "Hey, you. You haven't even done anything this morning yet. What makes you think you get a carrot?" Crystal's response was to nudge the other pocket in quest for more of her favorite treat. Kelly laughingly pushed her nose away. "If I don't watch out, you're going to be the next spoiled brat around here."

"I don't think you'll ever have to worry about that. Crystal knows she's loved, but she also knows what her limits are. That horse is as gentle as they come."

Kelly looked up as Granddaddy walked up from the house. "Good morning."

"Good morning, Kelly. I thought I'd come over and watch the show. Jason will turn out to be a fine horse if we can teach him some manners, but I must admit he's more spoiled than I expected. It's a shame, really. It's not his fault he's been made dangerous. I wish people could understand that discipline and firmness is not cruelty."

Mandy walked up with the troubled gelding. The look in his eyes told Kelly he knew something was up, and he wasn't interested in being a part of it. He snorted and rolled his eyes as Mandy approached the tying post, but Kelly couldn't detect any fear. He just seemed to not like the idea.

"I should have tied him to the tying post in the first place," Granddaddy said. "I just never thought that he hadn't learned even the basic things. He won't be able to pull that one up. I set that post myself about ten years ago. There's only five feet above the ground, but that post is sunk down into four feet of concrete. It's made of solid cedar and is ten inches in diameter. He can fight it all he wants. It's not going anywhere!" Stepping forward, he inspected the gelding closely. "Good, Mandy. You put the leather halter on him. It's nice and thick. And strong. I don't want him to be able to break it, but I also don't want him to burn or hurt his head. This should do the job. Go ahead and tie him up."

Mandy complied with Granddaddy's command and attached the short lead line hanging from the post to Jason's halter, all the while talking soothingly to the nervous gelding. As long as she stood next to him, he seemed content to remain standing. Turning his head, he saw Crystal standing calmly and seemed to relax a little.

"Okay. Walk away, and let's see what he does." Granddaddy's voice was calm and matter-of-fact.

Mandy stepped back and away from Jason. Jason took one step back, as if he had decided he had stood in that particular spot long enough. Finding himself unable to leave, he immediately lunged back against the rope. The rope held strong. Kelly then witnessed the fight of her life. Jason jumped backward until he jolted to a standstill. Then he lunged forward until his head almost rammed the post. The lunging and bursts continued for several minutes, until one desperate pull threw him to the ground. He lay panting for breath with his head straining against the rope holding him.

Granddaddy's voice was tight. "He's worse than I thought. I'll get him up. Mandy, go get the harness."

Mandy disappeared into the barn. Kelly spoke up. "The harness?"

Granddaddy approached the downed gelding carefully while he spoke. "Yep. This fellow needs to learn he can't fight this thing. But I don't want him to get hurt doing it. One thing I know for sure—he's not afraid. He's just too used to having his own way. The harness is a wide web belt that I've padded with sheepskin. It's basically a large lasso that I'm going to put around his girth area. The end will run up between his legs and through the bottom ring in his halter. We'll then attach it to the post. When he fights being tied, he will find himself cutting off his air supply. He'll release the tension just so he can breathe. It shouldn't take him too long to figure out he will feel much better if he just learns to stand there like a sane animal. We'll leave him for the two hours before class and then put him away. A few days of this lesson, and he should stand tied very nicely."

Releasing the rope holding Jason, Granddaddy allowed him to struggle to his feet. The gelding was shaking but unrepentant. His first act was to try and snap at Granddaddy's hand. His only reward for the effort was a sharp cuff to the nose. Jason rolled his eyes but submitted to standing there quietly.

Kelly shook her head. Jason's owners had definitely done him no favors. Come to think of it, she figured, they had made it hard on everyone involved with this beautiful, but stubborn, animal. Mandy appeared, and together she and Granddaddy put on the harness while Kelly watched closely. When they were finished, she was sure she could do it on her own if need be.

Once again Mandy stepped back and the fireworks began. Jason lunged back against the rope until he stood gasping for air. Then he jumped forward and waited a few moments before repeating the same shenanigans. It took him only ten minutes, though, to figure out that no matter how hard he tried, he was losing the battle. Finally, he stood still, his sides heaving. Every few moments he tugged lightly with his head, but he quit fighting— for the time being.

Granddaddy nodded in approval. "At least he's not stupid. He'll learn. It will just take a while. We'll leave him here for a couple of hours. Kelly, do you mind leaving Crystal tied? It will help keep him calm and show him that other horses don't freak out over this type of thing."

"Sure, Granddaddy," Kelly said. "I promised Mandy I would help her feed this morning, then we're going to have breakfast before the classes start showing up. I'll put both of them away after we eat."

• • •

Kelly leaned against the post and allowed her thoughts to wander. She had already done her two beginner classes that morning and had twenty minutes before the first of her two intermediate classes. There was plenty of time to dream about Greg, to remember every detail of their time together last night: *The Drawbridge, his approval of her dress, the fun of the dance, floating during the slow dances, being held in his arms as they talked into the early morning hours.* Her father had looked out the window once. Seeing Greg's car in the driveway thirty minutes before curfew, he had only waved.

Kelly could still hardly believe she was Greg Adams's girlfriend. She knew she was the envy of half the school, but that didn't really matter to her.

She was enjoying the friendship they shared. She was really glad they had talked about the physical aspect of their relationship. Setting limits and boundaries would protect their friendship.

"Hi, Kelly. Are you finding animals in the clouds or just lost in thought?"

"Oh, Mrs. Morgan. I guess I'm lost in thought." Looking at her watch she grinned. "I guess I was *very* lost in thought." Turning around, she laughed to see her entire class standing there watching her. They laughed too as they saw her face turn red. "Okay, well it looks like everyone is here. What do you say we get started?" Speaking quickly, Kelly assigned each rider a horse. "Go get them out of their stall and bring them out here. Once you get here, I want you to check all your tack and make sure it's right. I'll come around and check everyone before you get on."

The class scattered as they moved toward the barn. Kelly stood chatting with parents for a few minutes while the riders reappeared with their horses and set to work inspecting tack. Soon the air was filled with comments and chuckles.

"My stirrups are on upside down!"

"One of my reins is detached from my bridle!"

"Hey, this bridle is too loose. It's just hanging in Sugar's mouth!"

Kelly laughed as the inventory continued. They were catching on. It had taken her time to sabotage all the tack, but she knew it was worth the effort. The best way to learn how to do something right was to see it done wrong and then have to figure out how to fix it.

"My girth is hanging by one strap on the right side!"

"My saddle pad is bunched up under the saddle!"

The next twenty minutes were busy as she went around showing how to adjust bridles and saddles. As she worked with her students, she made each one explain what was wrong and why it needed to be fixed. It wasn't enough to know something was wrong. She also wanted them to be able to tell her *why* it was wrong. She could still remember her class session when Mandy had played this trick on her. It had been funny, but she had learned so much. By the time everyone was done, Kelly was sure they were convinced of the importance of checking all their tack before getting on their horses.

Satisfied with their groundwork, Kelly smiled, "Okay, everyone. Mount up. Then take a few minutes to walk your horses and get them warmed up. As the days get chillier it's important to make sure muscles are warm before you ask your horses to do much. They're like we are in that respect. Ask too much of cold muscles and you can end up with strains and swollen joints."

Kelly gave them about five minutes to walk around the ring. She called out instructions as they did. "Just because you're walking doesn't mean your horse can just slouch along. It's important to keep them alert and ready for your every command. Jamie, Sugar looks like she is ready to fall asleep on you. That's not exactly the way to warm up muscles! I want you to take up on your reins some so you have more contact with her mouth. Then I want you to give her some more leg. You need to get her attention and pick her body up with more leg pressure.

As you move her forward with your legs, she will meet the resistance of the bit. You don't want her to break into a trot. You just want to collect her some and make her wake up."

Kelly watched carefully as Jamie followed her instructions. She was glad to see the other class members working to accomplish the same thing. "Good! Doesn't that feel much better? It's not really a lot of fun to ride a sack of potatoes, is it?"

Jamie laughed. "You're right, Kelly. This does feel a lot better!"

"Okay, now everyone is awake, let's work some more on the sitting trot," Kelly called. "I can't tell you how important it is to be balanced on your horse. If you can learn to feel how they move and learn to move with them, you'll be able to ride any horse you get on. That's one reason I make each of you ride a different horse each week. It's easy to become comfortable and familiar with one horse, but if you want to be a good rider, you need to be able to ride anything."

Checking to make sure the riders were sufficiently spread out, she gave her next command. "Let's move them into a trot now. Remember what I told you a few weeks ago?"

Jamie smiled. "You mean about belly dancing? How could we forget that? I demonstrated for my father after dinner that night. He thought it was pretty weird!"

Kelly groaned. "Oh great! Now I'm going to get a reputation for weirdness. But the bottom line is— does it work?"

The class all laughed and agreed it did. Based on their performance that morning, it definitely was working. Kelly was thrilled at how far they had come in such a short time. She knew several of them were hoping to start jumping soon. They would be ready when Mandy had room in her classes.

Kelly finished up the class by allowing each rider to canter a few rounds of the arena. Whenever possible, she liked to focus on her students individually so she could best tell them how to improve. It was easy to miss fine points when she was watching ten to fifteen at a time, so she was careful to give everyone a few minutes of focused attention in each class.

The second class passed just as quickly as the first one. It was a good thing. Kelly was beginning to feel the strain of her fatigue. She was having fun, but she could definitely tell she had only gotten four hours of sleep. Getting to the barn at six-thirty and going non-stop for six hours had drained her. She could hardly wait to eat some lunch and then curl up in the hay barn and take a nap. She felt her body relax at the thought. Finding a pile of hay warmed by the sun and snuggling down into its depths was one of her favorite things to do. If only Greg could be there! Kelly knew he was working with his father for the morning, but they had made plans to go riding together at three. That would give her time for a nap so she would be refreshed and ready.

•   •   •

Full from lunch, Kelly wandered over to the hay barn. Mandy had promised to not let anyone disturb her for at least an hour. Slipping in through the metal gate, she looked around for the perfect spot.

It didn't take her long to find it. On the right side of the barn, about eight feet up, where she could overlook the lake, Kelly saw a pile of hay bales illuminated by the sun. Climbing up, she collapsed in a heap. Allowing herself to luxuriate in the warmth of the sun, she took off her jacket, rolled it into a pillow, and stuffed it under her head. Within minutes she was sound asleep.

Kelly, you look wonderful tonight.

Thank you, Greg.

Kelly smiled up at her handsome escort as he took her in his arms and began to move gently to the music.

"Kelly!"

Laying her head on his broad chest, she allowed herself to be led around the dance floor.

"Kelly! Wake up!"

Struggling to emerge from her world of dreams, Kelly mumbled and cracked open one eye. "Huh? Greg. What are you doing here? Is it already three?" Her voice was working, but Kelly refused to move from the warm cocoon she had created for herself. "Is it time for me to get up already? I feel like I just went to sleep."

"You did, Kelly. But I need to talk to you."

"Right now?"

"Right now."

The grimness and concern in Greg's voice finally broke through the fog of Kelly's sleepiness. Sitting up, she stretched and shook her head in an effort to wake up. "Is everything okay, Greg? What are you doing here?"

Satisfied she was awake enough to understand him, Greg took both of her hands and spoke gently. "There's been an accident, Kelly."

T W E L V E

I t's Emily, Kelly. She's been hit by a car."

Kelly felt herself begin to shake as Greg spoke. The world seemed to spin. Fear caused her voice to crack. "Emily? What happened? Is she okay?" Jumping up, she began to climb down the pile of hay bales.

Greg grabbed her hand to help her. "I don't really know, Kelly. Your father called just before they left for the hospital..."

"The hospital? Emily is in the hospital?" Frantically, Kelly fumbled with the chain on the barn gate.

Reaching down, Greg unlatched it and led her through. "Yes, the hospital. Your father called just before they left and asked me to come out and get you. They were following the ambulance over."

Kelly's voice broke in alarm. "An ambulance..."

"Your father didn't tell me much. They were in a hurry. All I know is that Emily was on her bike and got hit by a car. We'll know more when we get there. The hospital isn't too far from here. It won't take long."

155

Kelly could no longer control the shaking of her body. She said nothing else as Greg led her across the pasture to his car in the parking lot where both Mandy and Granddaddy caught her close in warm hugs. She was quiet as Greg broke all speed laws making it to the hospital. Her first words came when she saw her father striding down the hall toward her. Breaking free of Greg's hand, she ran to him and grabbed hold.

"How is she, Dad? What happened? Is she going to be okay?" Kelly didn't even try to control the shaking in her voice. All she wanted to do was hold onto her father and absorb his strength.

Her father held her close and stroked her rigid back. "We're still waiting for the doctors, honey. We don't know anything yet."

He held her for a few minutes and then released her to lead her down the hallway toward the waiting room. As he did, he spoke to Greg. "Thanks for picking her up, Greg. That was a big help."

Greg's response was quick. "I was happy to do it, Mr. Marshall. Besides, I want to know how Emily is, too. Do you know what happened?"

"We're beginning to piece it together," Kelly's dad replied. "Emily and her friend Shannon were riding their bikes in the neighborhood a few streets over. They were coming down a big hill and were going pretty fast when they went through the inter-section at the bottom. A car coming the other direc-tion didn't see them and decided to run the stop sign. Shannon said Emily saw the car and tried to stop, but she was going too fast. She hit the front of the car and flew over it headfirst." Kelly's dad's voice became thick and muffled. "She's been unconscious ever since. A neighbor saw what happened and called Peggy and me immediately, so we were there when the paramedics showed up. The doctors have been with her for about an hour."

Kelly's voice was still shaking but had begun to take on a dead tone as she struggled with her emotions. "Dad...will she...I mean...will she..." Kelly couldn't bring herself to voice her fears.

Her father took a deep breath. "I honestly don't know what to tell you. I wish I did. I'm believing she's going to be okay, but I don't know for sure. We'll all just have to wait."

When they arrived in the waiting room, Kelly looked around the too-familiar place. The week before her mother had died, she had been in this room every day, waiting between visits, in order to spend as much time as possible with her mom. It hadn't changed much. There were still the same pale green walls. Still the same placid, scenic pictures adorning the walls. Still the same dark green sofas and chairs with wooden arms. The only thing that had changed was the carpet. The beige carpet had been pulled up and replaced with a soft cream-colored one. Kelly couldn't believe she was back again. What would she do if Emily...?

Greg broke into her thoughts. "Can I get you anything, Kelly? There's a drink machine around the corner. Would you like a cola or something?"

Kelly nodded absently. "Whatever," she responded flatly.

Peggy and her father exchanged concerned looks. Sitting down next to her, her father took both of her cold hands in his. "Kelly. Don't imagine the worst yet. We still don't know anything. We have to just pray and trust God to take care of Emily. I'm concerned, too, but God has given me a real peace."

Kelly nodded again absently but found no words to respond. Sitting in this room was bringing back so many memories. Her mother steadily losing weight until she looked like a skeleton, trying valiantly to smile and let Kelly know she loved her. The agony Kelly had felt as the casket had been lowered into the ground. She was struggling to trust God, but her fears were winning.

Greg returned with the drink and placed it in her hand. At the same time, a man dressed in navy dress pants, a white shirt, and a colorful tie stepped around the corner.

"Mr. and Mrs. Marshall? I'm Doctor Harler. I'm taking care of your daughter."

Kelly continued to sit where she was as her father and Peggy strode forward to meet the pleasant-looking man. Her father reached out to grip the doctor's hand. "How's Emily?"

"Emily is one very lucky girl, Mr. Marshall," Dr. Harler replied. "She has a fairly serious concussion, but the helmet she was wearing probably saved her from a very critical head injury. The concussion is what caused her prolonged unconsciousness, but she came around a few minutes ago."

Kelly watched her father draw a deep breath of relief.

The doctor continued, "While the concussion is her most serious problem, she also broke her left arm. It was a fairly clean break. They are casting it right now. Six weeks or so and we should be able to take it off. She also has a fair share of cuts and bruises from her impact with the pavement. They will be painful for a while, but they should all heal nicely. Right now, I think she just wants to see her family. She asked for you as soon as she regained consciousness. Do you have any questions before I take you back to see her?"

"How long do you think she'll have to stay here?" Kelly's dad asked.

"At least until tomorrow afternoon. We want to monitor her and make sure it's not worse than we think it is. If she's doing well, we'll send her home. She'll get well quickest there. I'll make sure the nurses give you all the instructions you'll need to take good care of her. The most important thing for the next few days is for her to get plenty of sleep and rest. It will take the head a while to recover from the shock of such a serious impact." Turning, Dr. Harler headed down the hallway.

Minutes later, Kelly stood staring down at her sleeping sister. Her head hadn't gotten any cuts, but bandages covered a large portion of the rest of her body and her left arm was encased in fresh plaster. She seemed to be resting well. Dr. Harler, after speaking some instructions to the nurse, shook hands with her father and Peggy once more and then slipped out of the room. Kelly could not take her eyes off her sister. What if...?

Emily's eyes fluttered open. Smiling weakly, she held out her right hand to her father.

He grasped it warmly. Leaning over, he gave her a kiss. Kelly couldn't miss the tears welling up in his eyes.

"Hi, Dad." Emily's voice was faint but steady.

"Hi, Em. How do you feel?"

"My head hurts pretty bad. What happened?"

Mr. Marshall filled Emily in on the details of the accident.

"You're going to be okay, Em," he said gently. "The doctor says you need to stay here overnight, but I'll be right here with you. If you're good and do everything the nurses say, you might be able to go home tomorrow."

Emily nodded slightly at her father's words, gave a weak smile, and slipped once more into a deep sleep. Her father straightened up and made no effort to hide the tears in his eyes.

Kelly could feel her control slipping. Her fear had been replaced by surging emotions. Seeing Emily like that...being back in the waiting room ...watching the doctor stride up...the memories threatened to overwhelm her. Choking back her tears, she turned to flee from the room.

"Kelly?" Her escape was halted as her father reached out to take her arm.

Taking a deep breath, Kelly struggled for control but lost the battle when her father pulled her close to him in a warm hug. All the fears and hurts boiled over as she clung to him, sobbing. Her body shook uncontrollably as he attempted to soothe her. She knew he was speaking, but none of his words were registering. The sobs continued to spill out.

Gradually, as the sobs lessened, she was able to hear her father's voice.

"Emily is going to be okay, honey. She's going to be all right."

Kelly nodded her head as she choked out, "I know..."

"Then why are you crying, honey?"

All Kelly could do was shake her head. How could she explain the turmoil boiling inside her? Taking deep breaths, she brought the sobs under control and tried to stop shaking.

Her father continued to hold her, but she knew he was puzzled.

"Kelly's had a long day, Scott. Why don't we let Greg take her home? There's no need for her to stay any longer. Emily will sleep most of the night." Peggy's voice was soft in the background.

Suddenly Kelly remembered Greg's presence. He must think she was nuts! she thought. How could she have lost control like that with him around? Pulling away from her father, Kelly straightened and wiped her eyes with the tissue he offered. But Greg wasn't in the room.

Peggy answered the question in her eyes. "Greg slipped out a few minutes ago."

Kelly was relieved and also amazed at how perceptive he was. He had known she wouldn't want him to see her like that.

"He said he would wait outside until you were ready to leave." Peggy exchanged glances with her husband. "Your father is going to stay here all night. I'll be home about ten, after visiting hours are over. We gave Greg some money to take you out for dinner. I think a good meal will help you feel better." Peggy smiled gently. "Martin called before you got here to check on Emily, and he said he would stop by to pick you up for church in the morning, if you wanted to go. You just need to give him a call." Peggy's tone was tender and caring.

So much of Kelly yearned to reach out to her stepmother. She knew in her head that Peggy could give her the love and understanding she had so longed for since her mother's death. But the sight of Emily in bed, the horror she had felt when she'd heard about the accident, the memories threatening to overwhelm her. She couldn't take the risk. She *wouldn't* take the risk. The walls held firm as she nodded and turned to walk from the room.

• • •

Kelly was barraged with questions about Emily the next morning as she made her way from the parking lot to Sunday school. Martin was just finishing the opening prayer when she finally walked through the door.

"... and Lord, we thank you again for protecting Emily and keeping her from being more seriously hurt. We pray her recovery will be complete and quick. In Jesus' name. Amen."

Martin looked up and smiled as Kelly took her seat. He and Janie had made a special trip to her neighborhood to pick her up. Peggy had left early that morning to head back to the hospital and relieve Kelly's father.

Martin turned his attention back to the group. "I have a special surprise for you this morning. Some of y'all know Beth Myers. She graduated from Kingsport High two years ago and is now a sophomore at North Carolina State. She's in town for the weekend and came by to see me. We spent some time talking about what God has been putting on my heart the last few weeks, and she shared some things with me that I think you'll be interested in hearing. Come on up, Beth."

Beth Myers made her way to the front of the classroom. She wasn't exactly pretty, Kelly thought, but there was a warmth about her that made her attractive. Straight brown hair framed a somewhat angular face, but her glowing brown eyes spoke of a love for life. She cleared her throat and began to speak.

"When Martin, Janie, and I were talking last night over dinner, he mentioned what y'all had talked about in Sunday school a few weeks ago—about learning to let down the walls you've built in your life. It's been hard for me to learn that lesson. There are still days I struggle with it, but I'm doing much better.

"My parents split when I was very young. I remember walking around my front yard that day and crying. I believed if I let my folks know how much I was hurting, my dad would come back. When he didn't, I decided that I would never cry again. I would never let anyone know how I really felt because it didn't matter anyway. Age six is young to make that decision, but I was serious and I did it. I never cried, and no one knew who I really was. Oh, I was popular I guess. I was an athlete and involved in a lot of clubs, but none of my friends had any idea what I really thought or felt. No one had any idea that I was dying inside. All they saw was a laughing, carefree person. I had built my walls well, and I was very comfortable with them."

Beth stopped and smiled whimsically. "At least as comfortable as you can be while you're living a lie. I felt safe behind my walls, but inside I was crying out for someone to notice them, to tear them down, to show me love I could trust and depend on. Then I became a Christian. I knew Jesus had to be real because when I invited him into my life I cried for the first time in nine years. But I had no intention of letting down the walls I had built to protect myself from other people. God had other ideas, though. As he taught me about his love, he chipped away at my refusal to let other people love me. I was great at being a friend and giving love, but I couldn't accept it for myself. The poem Martin read a few weeks ago was one I wrote when I was seventeen."

Kelly nodded in remembrance. Her whole being was focused on what Beth was saying. Part of her wanted to shut it out; the other part of her drank in every word.

"Finally, God brought a very special friend into my life," Beth continued. "As soon as we met, I felt my heart unite with her. I don't know any other way to describe it. This person accepted me so completely and loved me just the way I was. I guess God knew the time was right. He gave me a trust for this person, and then the wall bashing started. Every time I would start to erect walls, this friend would say or do just the right thing. The combination of her love and the love of Christ finally brought the walls tumbling down.

"The freedom of no walls is incredible." Beth stopped and blinked the tears from her eyes. "I acknowledge the fact that I may get hurt in the

future. No human is perfect. Only God can meet all
our needs. But he puts people in our lives to love us
and be there for us. Martin described it really well
once. He said God puts people in our lives so we can
experience 'Jesus with flesh on.' God knows we need
to let people love us. It's part of the abundant life he
promises us. Your walls can only hurt you."

Kelly took a deep breath as Beth finished and sat
down. She knew Beth was speaking the truth. What
was she going to do about it?

• • •

Kelly came home from church to a blinking light
on the answering machine. Clicking it on, she heard
her father's voice.

"Well, Kelly, your sister has received the green
light from the doctor. He said it was amazing how
fast she's recovered. We're bringing her home! We
should be there about three. See you then."

Kelly clapped her hands and spun around in
delight. Emily was okay! Glancing at her watch, she
realized she had a little over an hour before they all
got home. There would be just enough time to run
to the video store and pick out a couple of her sister's
favorite movies. Checking the kitchen cabinets, she
found a bag of chocolate chips. If she hurried, she
could even have chocolate chip cookie dough made
and ready to pop in the oven for hot cookies during
the movies.

Running upstairs, she slipped out of her skirt and
sweater and hastily threw on a pair of jeans and a
bright green sweatshirt. Glancing outside at the

darkening clouds, she remembered the cold wind predicted for the afternoon. Pulling off the sweat-shirt, she put on a purple turtleneck and then re-placed the sweatshirt. The video store wasn't far, so she was going to walk. She had thought about taking her bike, but she knew it would be a while before she could ride it again. The memories of her sister's experience were still too fresh.

Just as she was passing through the kitchen on her way out the door, the phone rang. Kelly stopped to answer it. "Hello."

"Hi, Kelly. Did you hear from your father yet?"

Kelly smiled at hearing Greg's voice. "I had a message when I got home. Emily will be here in about an hour."

"That's great!"

"Yeah, it is. Listen, I'm running to the video store for a couple of movies, and then I'm going to make some cookies. Do you want to come over and watch the movies with us? I know Emily will need to get rest and not have a lot going on, but I also know she'd love to have you here."

"I'd love to come. Do you want me to pick up the movies?"

"No, thanks. It's a great day outside, and I'm feeling pretty cooped up after being in church this morning. I need some fresh air. It's almost two now. Why don't you come over about four? Emily will probably need some time to get settled in."

"You got it. See you at four."

Returning the phone to its cradle, Kelly grabbed some money out of the jar on the counter and headed out the door. It *was* a beautiful day. And she did need to get out and get some fresh air. Besides, she always did her best thinking outside. It gave her brain room to expand or something.

As she walked, her thoughts turned to the events of the day before. She had slept last night, but it had been restless because of the dreams invading her slumber. The dreams all ended the same: Emily was flying through the air over the hood of a car. When Kelly ran to Emily and turned her over, the face of her mother stared back at her.

"How's Emily, Kelly?"

Kelly was startled out of her dark thoughts by Nathan Sparks, a schoolmate of Emily's who lived down the road. "Oh, Nathan. Emily is doing fine. She has a bad headache, but she's coming home from the hospital in just a little while. The doctor says she's doing really well. I'll tell her you asked."

"Tell her I hope she comes back to school really soon."

"I'll do that, Nathan." Waving, Kelly continued on down the street. Several people stopped to ask about her sister. It seemed everyone knew about it. But then, Kelly considered, since it had just happened a few blocks away and the ambulance had come tearing down this street, everyone probably *did* know about it.

Kelly got back home just in time to make the cookies. Placing the two videos she had selected beside the VCR, she hurried into the kitchen and began mixing the dough. Emily loved her cookies. She would be thrilled Kelly had taken the time to do it. As far as Kelly was concerned, Emily was worth it. Kelly had realized afresh how much she loved her sister when she had seen her lying asleep in the big hospital room.

"We're home!"

Kelly had just slipped the dough in the refrigerator when the kitchen door swung open and her father walked in carrying Emily in his arms. Emily was laughing.

"Dad! You don't have to carry me, I tell you. I can walk!"

"I know you can, Em, so just relax and enjoy it. It's not often I get an excuse to pick up my baby."

Emily rolled her eyes, but looked pleased. "I'm not a baby, Dad! I'm almost twelve years old!"

"Yeah, I know, old woman! But you're still my baby and always will be!"

The laughter and teasing continued as he moved into the den. "As you requested, my daughter, you may stay down here for a while, but you're heading up to your room for sleep when you get tired."

"Yes, Dad." Emily's exaggerated patience erupted into a squeal when she saw the videos Kelly had picked out. "My two favorite movies! Where did they come from?"

Kelly stuck her head through the doorway and smiled. "Courtesy of the mean big sister. I figured you would be ready for some entertainment." Walking to the couch, Kelly leaned over to give Emily a big hug, careful of the bandages and cast.

"You bet I am! Thanks."

Kelly headed back to the kitchen to finish making the cookies. As she pulled the dough from the fridge, she heard a voice behind her.

"That was really nice of you, Kelly. Would you like me to bake those cookies for you?"

Kelly turned to find Peggy. She was surprised when a warm rush of love for her stepmother flooded her, but she kept her tone neutral. "That would be great, Peggy. The oven is turned on and ready."

Peggy nodded. "I'm going to get Emily settled in, and then I'll make the cookies while y'all watch the movie." She ran lightly up the stairs and returned moments later with a couple of blankets and enough pillows to make a fort.

Kelly laughed. "Emily will love all those pillows. She insists she can't sleep in her bed unless she's surrounded by them." As Peggy moved into the den where Emily was lying on the sofa, Kelly was struck by how considerate her stepmother was.

Standing at the door, Kelly watched Emily laugh as Peggy made a nest for her on the sofa. It was obvious how much Peggy and Emily loved each other. Kelly couldn't help the feelings of jealousy that surged through her. Her little sister responded so naturally to her stepmother. Why couldn't she do that? Why must the memory and pain of her mother's death create a wall she could not tear down? With a sigh, Kelly turned to answer the knock at the kitchen door.

"Come on in, Greg." Kelly was surprised at the frigid burst of air that blew in as she opened the door. "Boy! They were right about a cold front coming through today. I'm glad we're not out in a boat for *this* one!"

Greg laughed. "You got that right. They would be scraping ice bodies off the bottom of the boat!" Tossing his jacket onto the counter, he sniffed.

"Where's the cookies?" He made no attempt to hide the disappointment in his voice.

Kelly pretended hurt. "Is that the only reason you're here? Cookies?"

"Well, no... but it makes being with you even sweeter."

Kelly groaned. "Save me the one-liners, please. What have you been doing? Reading a book or something?"

Greg laughed along with her but continued to search the kitchen with his eyes.

Kelly pushed him toward the den. "Go in there and say hi to Emily. We're going to start watching the movie while Peggy puts in the first batch of cookies. The dough is all ready."

Greg headed to the bowl of dough on the counter and gave Kelly a mock pleading look. "Is there a penalty if I steal cookie dough? I like them cooked, but I *really* like the raw dough."

Kelly laughed. "You and my father. I honestly don't even know why we bother to cook them. Help yourself. When you're through being a pig, you can come join us for the movie." With those final words, she disappeared through the swinging door into the den.

Greg appeared moments later with a large clump of dough on a spoon. His words were muffled around a full mouth. "Emily! Sure is good to see you home. Do I get to be the first to sign your cast?"

"Sure! I want you and Kelly to be the first ones. There are some colored pens over in the desk drawer. Would you mind getting them for me? Dad and Peggy have threatened death if I get off the sofa."

Emily laughed at Peggy who stuck out her tongue as she exited the den. Once again, Kelly was struck by a wave of longing. To hide her emotion, she busied herself getting the movie in and cued up. She and Greg both signed the cast, and then they settled down on big throw pillows in front of the sofa where Emily was lying.

They were just finishing the first movie when her father came striding in with an armful of wood. Kelly started to speak, but her dad held his fingers to his lips in a gesture for silence. Seeing Kelly's questioning look, he pointed toward the sofa. Turning, she discovered her sister was sound asleep. Her father quietly laid the fire and then he, Kelly, and Greg slipped from the den into the kitchen.

Peggy was just pulling the final tray of cookies from the oven. A hard wind rattled the windows of the kitchen, but warmth radiated through the room. The rich aroma of the cookies filled the air as Kelly and Greg sat down at the kitchen table. Her father poured glasses of milk as Peggy set a large plate of cookies in front of them.

Greg grunted his appreciation as he bit into one of the soft, chewy morsels. Scott Marshall followed suit, and for a while there was silence as the four of them dug into the mountain of cookies before them.

"Wonderful as usual, Kelly."

"Thanks, Dad. By the way, how long before Emily can go to school? Shannon called and said she would be happy to bring her books and homework assignments home."

"That's good. The doctor said she should be feeling a lot better by tomorrow but to not let her go to school until Friday. She had a pretty nasty blow to the head, and he wants to be extra careful. She'll probably be bored to death in a couple of days, but we're going to follow his orders."

Kelly nodded. "I've got some books on my shelves she's been wanting to read. I'll get them for her."

Emily's voice from the other room announced she was awake again. Grabbing the plate of cookies, they all moved into the den and settled down for the next movie.

• • •

Kelly sat on the window seat and stared out at the tossing leaves. The wind was still blowing hard. With Emily safe at home, Kelly didn't care what the weather did. She was ready for a season of roaring fires, anyway.

Thoughts of the last two days roamed through her mind. She was tired, but she was almost afraid to go to sleep. The dreams of last night still haunted her mind. Now that there was nothing to distract her, the reality of what she had been dreaming flooded her. Try as she might, she could not wipe the image of her mother's face from her mind. She finally gave up and crawled into bed, hoping that sleep would offer some relief.

She was still wide awake when Peggy cracked open the door and looked in.

"Kelly?" Her voice was soft.

Kelly opened her mouth to ask her to please come in, but closed it again quickly. Squeezing her eyes shut, she pretended to be asleep. Peggy stood there a second, turned to leave, then turned back. Walking across the room to where Kelly lay, she leaned down and kissed her on the forehead gently. Straightening, she slipped from the room.

Kelly lay there quietly as tears flowed down her face.

THIRTEEN

How's Emily? Didn't you tell me she was supposed to go back to school today?"

Kelly smiled at Julie as she slipped into the desk next to hers. They were just minutes from another algebra test, but Kelly felt ready for it this time. "Yeah. She went back this morning. I'm not sure who was happier—her or Peggy. Emily's been going stir-crazy. At first, she was content to just lie around. If she tried to get up, she'd get really dizzy, and she had a lot of nightmares. She's doing a lot better now, though. By Wednesday Peggy could hardly keep her in bed. Finally, Peggy let Emily come into the kitchen, and she taught her how to make bread and cakes and stuff. Said it was the only way she could keep her mostly still. I'm sure the neighbors are happy, though. Emily went around last night and delivered all of the goodies they made!"

Julie smiled and then laughed out loud as Kelly pulled out a foil-wrapped package from her book bag and grinned. "Except for this one, of course," Kelly added. "I knew we would need brain power for our test, so I snatched a bunch of peanut butter brownies for us. They had so much stuff on the counter, I'm sure they never even missed it!"

She tossed the package to Julie who unwrapped it while Kelly finished talking. "Anyway, Emily is at school today. If I know my sister, she probably has her cast almost completely filled with signatures by now. And she's only been there an hour or so. She will definitely make the most of her celebrity position. She kept reminding me that now I was not the only Marshall girl who had a newspaper article written about her."

Julie laughed, stuffed a brownie in her mouth, and changed the subject. "Are you ready for this test?"

"I am, but more important, are *you?*"

"I am, thanks to you. I don't know what I would do if you weren't helping me with this stuff. You can actually make it make sense to me. That's quite an accomplishment with *my* brain." Grabbing another brownie, Julie turned to the front just as Mrs. Johnson stood from behind her desk.

Following suit, Kelly stuffed in a brownie, slipped one to Bernie, who had been eyeing her enviously, and rotated in her seat to face the front of the class.

"Those look great, Kelly. Did you bring enough for the whole class, or just enough for your favorite algebra teacher?"

Kelly turned red. Her mouth was too full to do more than mumble an incoherent reply to Mrs. Johnson's question. The whole class laughed, but Kelly didn't really mind. She knew her algebra teacher wasn't mad. Chewing quickly, she gave a big swallow and held out a brownie. "Do I get brownie points on my test if I give you one?"

Mrs. Johnson laughed at Kelly's impish grin. "Good try. I'm afraid you'll have to stand on your own merits, but I'll take a brownie anyway. They look great!" Stepping forward, she took the extended brownie, stuffed it in her mouth, and then proceeded to hand out tests.

The class continued to laugh, Kelly included. It was great to know that teachers could be fun, too. So many of them were serious all the time. She was glad Mrs. Johnson knew how to lighten up.

The morning flew by. Even with the brownies she had devoured, Kelly was starving when lunchtime came. There was something about cold, crisp fall weather that kept her hungry. Greg cocked an eyebrow when he saw her tray.

"Two slices of pizza, a hamburger, chips, and an ice cream sandwich?"

"I'm hungry," Kelly said in defense.

"*Hungry* is not the word for it. Where are you planning on putting all that?"

Kelly laughed in protest. "Hey, I'm a growing girl. I need my nutrition."

It was Greg's turn to laugh. "I have my doubts about any of that being nutrition, but it should at least fill up the empty pit you call a stomach."

Kelly stuck out her tongue, bowed her head for a quick blessing, and began to eat. Her mouth was too full to do more than mumble a greeting when Julie and Brent showed up with their trays. They, too, laughed at Kelly's full tray, but she shrugged them off. She was hungry, and she knew she didn't need to worry about her figure. She worked hard enough at the barn to burn off the excess calories.

Julie turned to Kelly. "What time are the guys picking us up tonight? And what are you going to wear?"

Kelly groaned. Greg looked up quickly.

"What's wrong, Kelly? Can't you go tonight?"

"Oh, sure! It's just that I forgot to mention it to my dad and Peggy. He has a late house showing tonight. That's why your dad is giving me a ride home from the stables this afternoon. Usually my dad wants to know what I'm doing in advance, but I'm sure he'll understand. It's been a crazy week with Emily getting hurt."

"Should we change it to tomorrow night?" Greg asked.

"No way. It'll be fine."

He nodded and turned back to discuss the soccer team's standing with Brent.

"I was planning on just wearing jeans tonight," Kelly said in answer to Julie's earlier question. "I bought a new sweater a couple of weeks ago to go with them."

The rest of lunch passed quickly as the four of them made plans for the night. By the time they were ready to head for fourth period, they had picked a movie to see and had also decided to go to Friendly's for ice cream afterward. On any Friday night you could count on it being jammed with Kingsport High students after ten. The owners liked their business, and there was never any trouble.

• • •

Kelly gave Crystal one more hug and then ran out of the barn just as Greg's father drove up. Greg appeared on Granddaddy's porch after having gone inside to pay his monthly board. They moved in unison to his father's car and climbed in.

"How'd it go today, kids?"

"Just great!" Kelly smiled at Mr. Adams. "Crystal and I had a good ride this afternoon. She took the right lead every time but one when we were cantering. And that brat, Jason, only tried to bite my hand once when I was grooming him. After only one swat he decided he would stand there and be a good boy."

Greg's father laughed. "I'm glad to hear that. Greg told me about Jason and some of his antics. Is he tying now, too?"

"He doesn't bother to act like he likes it," Greg spoke up, "but he's quit fighting it. Kelly even cross-tied him in the aisle today, and he acted like a gentleman. He really is a beautiful horse. It looks like he might develop a personality to match his looks. Granddaddy says things are going well."

The rest of the ride home was spent happily discussing how the day had gone.

Bursting into the warmth of the kitchen, Kelly was struck by how tired Peggy looked. She knew it must have been a hard week for her. She had taken care of Emily Monday through Thursday, and then had worked in the real estate office for several hours today.

Peggy looked up from the oven and gave a weary smile. "Your father won't be here for dinner. It should be ready soon. I was a little late getting home."

Kelly nodded. "You look tired."

Peggy seemed a little surprised she had noticed but nodded. "I am, I suppose. It's been a long week. I think I must be coming down with a cold or something. On top of that, I had a couple of friends call me today with some pretty serious problems. I'm glad it's the weekend."

Kelly moved toward the cabinets. "How about if I set the table for you?"

Again, Peggy registered surprise but spoke gratefully. "I'd appreciate that. Usually Emily takes care of that for me, but I made her go upstairs and take a nap. She was really worn out after her first day back at school. Once you set the table, would you mind waking her up? She needs to eat something."

"I'll be happy to." Kelly was surprised how good her helpful attitude felt. There hadn't been much open conflict lately between her and Peggy, except for the boat incident, but Kelly knew she was very distant to her stepmother.

It only took a few minutes to set the table, and then Kelly went upstairs to wake her sister. Emily was sleeping soundly. Kelly shook her gently on the shoulder. "Hey, Em. It's time to wake up, sleepyhead. Dinner is almost ready."

Emily cocked open one sleepy eye and drowsily rose on one elbow. "Hey, Kelly. Look at my cast. Isn't it cool?" Her words were slurred with sleep.

Kelly sat down on the edge of the bed and inspected the extended cast. She had been right—Emily had it full of signatures. Kelly could barely see white under the maze of names and pictures that crisscrossed in all colors. "It's definitely cool, Em. You ready to eat?"

Emily swung her legs out of the bed in response. "I'm always ready to eat. I'm glad Peggy made me sleep, though. I was pretty beat. I guess I'm not quite back to normal yet."

"Whatever normal is. I don't know that you were *normal* before the accident." Kelly laughed as she threw out the teasing words and then ducked to miss the cast Emily was swinging toward her head.

Still laughing, they clambered down the stairs to the kitchen. Peggy had just pulled the pizza from the oven. She poured drinks while Kelly retrieved the salads from the refrigerator and unearthed two different kinds of dressing. Settling down, Kelly dug into the meal in front of her.

"Emily got me to rent a couple of videos for tonight," Peggy said pleasantly. "I think you'll like the ones I picked out."

Kelly stopped a forkful of salad in midair. "Uh, I won't be here tonight. Greg is coming to pick me up in about an hour."

Peggy lowered her own fork. "Where are you going?"

"Oh, just to the movies. And then to Friendly's for ice cream. We should be home around eleven."

Peggy spoke slowly. "Does your father know about this? He didn't say anything to me."

"Well, no." Kelly felt her first twinge of uneasiness. "I meant to tell him earlier in the week, but with everything going on, I forgot. I'm sure it's okay."

"It probably is, but I know your father likes to know in advance. Are you sure it's such a good idea to go?"

Kelly could feel her frustration rising. She didn't know why Peggy was making such a big deal out of it. She knew her father wouldn't mind her going. She also knew her voice was getting tight. "I'm sure it's fine, Peggy." The look of caution on Peggy's face caused Kelly's anger to boil.

Peggy's voice became a little more firm. "I'm not sure I agree with you. I know how your father feels about it. He should be home in an hour and a half. Why don't you wait and ask him?"

Kelly's voice rose as she responded. "An hour and a half? The movie will have started by then! We won't get in to see it, and there's not another one we want to see!" Her earlier feelings of compassion for Peggy fled. "You can't make me stay here!"

Peggy's face tightened as she opened her mouth to respond.

Kelly didn't give her a chance. Jumping up from the table, she threw down her fork and shoved back her chair. All the emotions she had tried too hard to control spewed out. "Look. I keep telling you, you're not my mother. I don't know why you want to try and act like it! Why don't you just leave me alone? Dad wouldn't make a big deal out of me going to the movies. I don't know why you have to. I'm *going* to the movies!" Spitting out the final words, she turned and ran up the stairs. She was dimly aware of tears rolling down Emily's stricken face as she fled past her.

It took just a few minutes for Kelly to change into some clean jeans and the new sweater she had told Julie about at lunch. She grabbed a warm jacket and then waited at the top of the stairs until she was sure Peggy and Emily had moved into the den for their movies. Soundlessly she slipped down the stairs and out the kitchen door. There was no point in there being another scene. She was already sorry for the blowup, but she was still angry at her stepmother. She had no business trying to run her life, Kelly fumed. Who did she think she was?

Kelly had thirty minutes to wait before Greg was supposed to pick her up. She was grateful for the warmth of the jacket as she pulled it close around her. Seeking the comfort of familiarity, she walked over to her sentinel oak. Leaning back against its strong solidity, she gazed up at the sky. Gone were the twinkling stars that sang to her on so many nights. In their place were dense clouds scudding across the sky, trying to escape the brisk wind pursuing them. The clouds were low enough for the lights of the city to reflect off of them. They seemed to dance and swirl as they changed from light gray to charcoal to dense ebony. Occasionally she would be offered a brief glimpse of the moon as it peeked through a window in the cover. Kelly allowed herself to be sucked up into the bubbling cauldron of the sky. It reflected her own turmoil perfectly.

She had been waiting only twenty minutes when she heard Greg's car approaching. Thank goodness he was early, Kelly thought. She didn't want to encounter her father until later. She was sure what his response would be to her latest blowup, but she had decided to go to the movies, and she was going! Jumping up, she ran lightly to the street where Greg would catch her in his headlights. As soon as he stopped, she opened the passenger door and jumped in.

"Hi!" She forced her voice to be light and cheerful.

"Hi, yourself. What are you doing out here?"

"Oh, it was such a nice night I decided to wait out here for you." Kelly felt a twinge of remorse at her lie, but she didn't let it stop her. "Peggy and Emily are watching a movie, so I thought it would be best if we didn't disturb them. And it really is a nice night. Did you see all the clouds? They're really something. They kept changing color, and they seem to be dancing around..."

"You're babbling."

Kelly stopped in the middle of her sentence. "Huh?"

Greg's voice was patient. "You're babbling. You only babble when something is bothering you. What's wrong?"

"Wrong? Nothing's wrong. Can't I just talk if I want to? Why do you have to call it babbling? Excuse me if I'm bothering you. I just won't talk anymore." Kelly heard her voice rising and was horrified. She didn't want to fight with Greg.

Greg turned and grabbed her hands. "Whoa, calm down. I don't mind your babbling. It's kind of cute. But you only do it when something is bothering you. I just wanted to know if I could help. Are you okay?"

Kelly hesitated in confusion. What could she tell him? She opted for partial truth. "I'm okay. It's just that Peggy and I kinda had a disagreement. I didn't feel like being in the house, so I came out here to wait for you."

"What were you fighting about?"

Kelly remained silent.

"Was it something to do with tonight?"

Kelly looked at him quickly. How could he be right so much of the time? "A little. She seemed to think I shouldn't go since I hadn't talked to my dad about it. I meant to—I just forgot with everything else going on this week. Besides, I know he won't mind."

Greg's voice was troubled. "A movie isn't worth fighting over. Why don't we call Brent and Julie and change it to another night? We can go inside and watch the movie with Peggy and Emily. I hate to see you fighting with Peggy."

Kelly could hear her voice rising again. "No way! We've made plans to go to the movie, and that's what we're going to do." Fighting to bring her voice under control, she continued in a more pleading tone, "Look. Everything will be fine. We just disagreed a little. I know my father won't mind if I go. And I *really* want to go. I need some fun after everything that happened this week." She could sense Greg was softening. She laid her hand on his arm. "Please, Greg."

He sat in silence for a few moments and then started the car. "I'm not sure I feel good about it, but you win. I hope I don't catch it from your father when we get back."

Kelly hastened to reassure him. "Everything will be fine. And we're going to have a great time tonight. Let's go get Brent and Julie."

As they drove off, Kelly looked back at the house just in time to see Peggy staring out the window. Kelly felt a pang of remorse, but she also experienced the thrill of victory.

• • •

"Kelly!"

"Greg!"

"Hi, Brent!"

"Julie! How's it going?"

Kelly smiled as a chorus of greetings surrounded them as soon as they pushed open the door to Friendly's Ice Cream Parlor. As usual, there were at least fifty Kingsport High students there. The four of them returned greetings and then slid into one of the few remaining empty booths.

Kelly picked up a menu and glanced at it idly, but she already knew what she wanted. She got the same thing every time she came—a Brownie Delight. They took a thick warm brownie and topped it with two scoops of chocolate chip ice cream, a generous ladle of hot fudge sauce, whipped topping, and two cherries. Her mouth drooled just thinking about it. As the other three studied the menu, she studied Greg. She had had so much fun at the movies with him tonight. He had been subdued at first. Kelly was sure he was thinking about her fight with Peggy, so she had determined to become the life of the party in order to take his mind off it. Her plan had succeeded. As she chattered—or babbled, as he called it—he gradually shook off his quietness and joined in. The movie they had selected was a comedy, and they had roared laughing all the way through. There were also a couple of touching scenes when Greg had pulled her close within his arm. She had been content to settle back and enjoy his closeness. The movie had ended too soon.

It was almost eleven when they dropped Julie and Brent off at their houses. Greg turned his car toward her neighborhood, but Kelly put her hand on his arm and stopped him.

"Let's go by the barn."

"Huh? It's eleven at night."

"I know, but it's such a beautiful night. I just want to see Crystal and give her an apple. I know you carry some in your trunk for Shandy. We won't stay long. Only a few minutes. My curfew isn't until eleven-thirty. Come on...just this once."

Greg shook his head and laughed. "Girl, you can talk me into more things! Porter's, here we come."

Continuing to laugh, he maneuvered the car in a U-turn and headed back the way they had come. In just moments they were cruising up the long drive to the stables. As they got closer to Granddaddy's house, Greg switched off the lights. "I'd hate to wake Granddaddy up. Besides, he'll think we're nuts if he knows we're out here at this time of the night!"

They were both quiet as they headed toward the barn. Slipping into the darkened corridor, they headed by remote control to their horses' stalls. Greg spoke quietly and was rewarded by a soft nicker from Shandy.

"Crystal," Kelly called softly.

Silence.

"Crystal. How are you, girl?"

Still no response.

Kelly felt uneasy as she drew near to the door of her filly's stall. She had always responded before. She became alarmed when she didn't see Crystal's head hanging out over the door. Where was her filly? Running the last few steps, she opened the

door and stepped in. There was just enough light to
outline the thrashing body of her sweat-glistened
horse.

Kelly's voice rose in a shrill scream.

FOURTEEN

Crystal!" Kelly flashed to her filly's side. "What's wrong, girl?" Her voice was frightened.

Within seconds Greg was in the stall with her.

Crystal moaned as she looked up at Kelly with anguished eyes. The beautiful filly was stretched out on the floor. As Kelly watched, she thrashed around in agony and then, moaning, lay back again. In spite of the cold, she was glistening with sweat. Her belly was swollen and bloated.

Colic! Kelly had never seen a case before, but she had heard plenty about it. Granddaddy had lost a horse two years ago that had colicked and died. Kelly groaned and jumped for the stall door.

"I'm going to get help." Tears were already running down her face as she ran back the way she had come.

"Granddaddy!" Kelly's frantic banging had brought him to the door.

"Kelly. What in the world is the matter with you, girl? What are you doing here? It's after eleven! And what are you crying for?" Granddaddy Porter opened the screen door and tried to pull her in, but Kelly grabbed his arm and tried to pull him out instead. She was frantic to get back to Crystal.

"It's Crystal! She's sick! I think it's colic. Granddaddy, you've got to help me!"

Granddaddy's features became grim, but his voice remained calm. Resisting her pull, he reached back inside to grab his heavy coat. Pulling it on over his overalls, he turned to join her. "Good thing I was still up. Whether it's colic or not, it's obvious she's sick by how afraid you are. Run in and call Mandy and tell her to come over and help me. Then call the vet. His number is by the phone. Tell him to come out as soon as possible."

Kelly wiped her tears away and ran to obey. At least she could do *something* to help her filly. Dialing Mandy's number, she waited impatiently for her to answer.

"Hello," Mandy answered sleepily.

"Mandy, it's me, Kelly. I'm in Granddaddy's house. Crystal is real sick. Granddaddy said to come over and help him. I have to call the vet." Kelly's voice broke into a sob, "Please hurry!"

Mandy asked no questions. "I'll be right there," she said and then hung up.

Shaking, Kelly managed to dial the vet's number. She was just glad to hear his gruff voice answer after only two rings.

"Dr. Shackleford, this is Kelly Marshall out at Porter's Stables. Crystal is sick. Real sick. I think it's colic. Can you please come out? I know it's late, but I'm really afraid . . ."

The vet spoke soothingly to the frantic girl. "What seems to be the problem? Can you tell me the symptoms?"

He listened silently, with the exception of a few grunts, as Kelly explained the condition she had found Crystal in.

"Yep, I believe you're right. Sounds like colic. I'm on my way. It will take me about twenty minutes. While you're waiting for me, see if you can get her on her feet. Get her walking, if possible. Either way, put a blanket over her so she'll stay warm. Do you know how long she's been down?"

"I have no idea. I just came out here to surprise her and found her sick." Kelly's voice rose in a wail again. "Please come quickly!"

"I'm on my way."

"Thanks, Dr. Shackleford."

Gulping back her sobs, Kelly raced toward the barn. Tearing down the corridor, she flung open the door to Crystal's stall, ready to follow the vet's instructions to the letter.

Greg and Granddaddy were kneeling beside her downed filly. Kelly caught her breath as she noticed the look of grim concern on Granddaddy's face. She fought to steady her voice.

"Dr. Shackleford said we needed to get her up. He said he'd be here in about twenty minutes."

Granddaddy nodded. "Yep. We're trying. She just doesn't seem to be interested. Where's Mandy?"

"She's on her way."

"Okay. Kelly, you come kneel by Crystal's head. I reckon she'll do anything for you. Greg, let's try to get her up again." Greg reached down for the lead rope he had fastened to the thrashing head and obligingly began to pull. At the same time Grand-daddy moved around behind Crystal and pushed against her straining body. Crystal's only response was a low moaning sound that escaped her flaring nostrils. She rolled her eyes and fell back as she continued to thrash on the floor.

The agony of her beautiful filly tore at Kelly's heart. Tears fell freely down her face as she tried to cradle Crystal's head. The thrashing of her body made it impossible.

Just then Mandy's head popped over the stall door. It took only a second for her to assess the situation. Her face became grave. Looking up, Granddaddy barked out more orders.

"Go get the red travel blanket. The thick one in the trunk. Greg, you go with her and get the hot water bottles out of the medicine cabinet. Go into my house and fill them with the hottest water you can. And hurry!"

Mandy and Greg disappeared. By now the barn was ablaze with light. All the other horses had their heads hanging over the stalls, wondering what in the world was going on.

"We need to keep trying to get her up, Kelly. She's going to be in trouble if she stays like this."

Kelly gulped and nodded. The tears had stopped. All of her attention was focused on her beloved filly. "Just tell me what to do, Granddaddy."

"Stay with her. When I tell you to, pull on her head and try to roll her up where she can get her feet underneath her."

Granddaddy disappeared. When he reappeared, Kelly was horrified to see a riding crop with a wide leather end in his hand. She had never touched Crystal with anything. Granddaddy saw Kelly's horror and hastened to reassure her, even though his tone was grim.

"I won't hurt her, Kelly. But we have to get her up. All this rolling around could cause her to rupture her intestines. If that happens, she's a goner."

Kelly only nodded. When Granddaddy gave the word, she stood and tugged hard at the thrashing black head. At the same time, Granddaddy lowered the crop on her hindquarters. Crystal's eyes widened further as she lunged upward and then fell back in agony. Her eyes pleaded with Kelly. It was no use. Crystal was not going to get up. Now all they could do was try to keep her warm until the doctor came.

Mandy appeared at the stall door with the blanket. Together, she and Granddaddy laid it across the distressed filly.

"She seems to be quieter now, Granddaddy," Kelly observed. "She's not moving around as much. Isn't that good?"

Granddaddy didn't say anything—just exchanged a grim look with Mandy.

Mandy moved over and put an arm around the shaking girl's shoulders. "It looks like she's going into shock, Kelly. The rolling is bad, but at least it indicates she's fighting. Just keep talking to her. It will help her to know you're here."

Greg appeared at the stall door. His arms were loaded with hot water bottles. Mandy reached up and handed them to Granddaddy as he placed them under the blanket on top of the sweating filly.

Mandy answered the question in Kelly's eyes. "We have to keep her warm. Especially if she's going into shock."

Kelly continued to stroke the filly's head and murmur to her. She was only vaguely aware of Greg's words.

"I called her folks. They're on their way out. They are calling my parents so no one will worry." Straightening, he glanced between a crack in the barn wall. "I see lights. It must be Dr. Shackleford. I'll go outside and get him."

Minutes later he ran back inside with the vet. Dr. Shackleford took one look and then turned to Greg. "Greg, you'll find a large black case in the rear of my truck. It says IV in big white letters. Get it and bring it to me immediately."

Greg disappeared as the vet turned back to the now-quiet filly. Kneeling beside her, he began his inspection. As he monitored her vital signs he spoke quietly. "Anybody know how this happened?"

Mandy spoke. "I have no idea. She was fine about six this evening. I fed the horses and then went over to my trailer."

The vet nodded. "No idea, then, how long she's been down like this?"

"No."

"Okay. Y'all did a good job getting the blankets and hot water bottles on her. I'm not surprised you couldn't get her up. She must have been down for a while. She's definitely gone into shock." His voice was grim, but he tried to look reassuring as he spoke to Kelly. "We're going to do the best we can, Kelly. She's in good shape. That will help her. We need to get some antibiotics in her to fight the shock."

Kelly's heart tore at the seriousness of his voice. This wasn't just a stomachache. What would she do if something happened to her filly?

Greg ran back into the barn with the case, and the vet motioned them all, except Mandy, to leave the stall. Greg helped Kelly to her feet. Supporting her with his arm, he led her out into the aisle. Kelly turned and leaned against the side of the stall as she watched the vet's activity. Dr. Shackleford pulled a portable stand out of the bag and erected it next to Crystal's body. He hung a full bag of intravenous solution from the post and then carefully inserted a needle into the filly's neck. Crystal gave no response. Moving quickly, he secured the needle with tape and then attached the tubing from the intravenous bag. Once the drip began, he settled back in the stall and continued to monitor her signs.

Kelly was vaguely aware of her father and Peggy entering the barn. She felt her father's arm around her waist, but she couldn't speak. She did nothing but stare at Crystal. She knew her filly was very sick. What if . . . ? Kelly could feel the familiar deadness creeping into her mind and body. She didn't notice the tears coursing down her face. She could dimly hear her father's voice, but his words weren't registering. She was hardly aware he was there.

The barn was quiet as the vet fought to save the sick filly. Greg slipped into the stall when the vet motioned him to take the hot water bags and refill them. Mandy placed the new ones under the blanket, and then they went back to watching the still filly. Crystal's only movement was a barely perceptible flutter of her nostrils. As Kelly watched, the expression on the doctor's face grew more and more grim. He exchanged a look with Granddaddy that spoke more than words ever could.

Unaware she had stopped crying, Kelly turned away from the scene. She could not bear to watch her beloved filly die. Stumbling, she started to walk down the aisle. Greg reached out to her, but she shrugged him away. She just wanted to be alone. He started to speak, but Peggy silenced him with a look. Continuing to stumble forward, Kelly found herself at the doorway overlooking the pasture. She vaguely resented the fact that the moon could shine on a night like tonight. The clouds had finally blown away before the relentless wind, and the sky was crystal clear.

As Kelly gazed over the pasture, all the memories and fears began to strangle her heart. Once more the images of her mother's last days and death appeared in her mind. Was her whole life going to be one of dealing with the deaths of those she loved most? Would it never end? What good was God if all the bad things continued to happen? Kelly gave a short sob and sagged against the barn. Unaware that anyone was with her, she was surprised when strong arms caught her from behind. She was even more surprised when the arms pulled her around into a strong embrace and she saw Peggy's face. Her whole body stiffened as she resisted the gesture.

"Kelly, I love you. I know what you're feeling. You've got to let all your pain go. Your walls are going to end up destroying you." Peggy's voice was gentle, but she didn't release the resistant girl.

Kelly was aware of a battle raging in her heart. Could she let this woman love her? Could she take the risk again? The pain she was feeling became more than she could bear alone. Breaking into wild sobs, she allowed Peggy to pull her close. Wrapping her arms around her stepmother, she laid her head against her chest and let the grief take control. She had no idea how long they stood there. Time didn't matter. As Kelly cried she thought about her mother and the pain of losing her. Wrapped in the love of her stepmother, Kelly was able to see the love of Jesus. It was as if he was crying tears with her. A healing had begun in Kelly's heart.

Gradually, Kelly became aware of Peggy's tears. This woman, who she had fought so hard against, was praying quietly for her. Grabbing Peggy even tighter, Kelly soaked up the closeness and allowed it to calm her heart. Whatever happened, she was through fighting Peggy. She needed her love. She wanted her love.

"Kelly!"

Kelly didn't move in response to Greg's voice. She wasn't ready to face the reality of the situation yet. She knew she would have to, but not quite yet.

"Kelly! Crystal is coming around. The antibiotics are working!"

What Greg said slowly filtered through Kelly's mind. Raising her head, she looked up in wonder. Greg's smiling face spoke louder than his words. "She's coming around, Kelly," Greg repeated. "Dr. Shackleford wants you to come talk to her. He said she'll respond to you better than anyone else."

Kelly gave Peggy a quick hug and sprang toward the stall. Flashing inside, she knelt beside her sick filly. Crystal was still down, but she was conscious.

Dr. Shackleford spoke with a quiet victory in his voice. "Her pulse is better, and her breathing is getting easier. Her mucus membrane has changed color from the muddy brown we saw earlier. We'll wait a little while, and then we'll try to get her up again. We're not out of the woods until she's standing up."

Kelly's tears started again as she spoke words of encouragement to her filly, but she didn't care. She wasn't going to try to stop the tears anymore. Kelly knew now that it was okay to cry when she was hurting. It was part of God's way of releasing pain. Her voice was surprisingly steady as she stroked Crystal's face. "You're going to make it, girl. Just a little while longer and then we'll get you up. You won't have to lie there under that blanket with a needle in you. We'll get you up, and then we'll take a long walk."

Mandy chuckled. "Don't tell her that. *We* know a long walk will make her feel much better, but I don't think *she's* going to be too excited about it."

The others standing around the stall laughed as the fear of death lifted from the barn. It was still going to be a long night, but the worst part was over. A cheer rose when Crystal raised her head and gave a soft nicker.

Dr. Shackleford waited another twenty minutes and then gave Kelly's dad and Greg orders to station themselves behind Crystal where they could help her up. He pulled out the IV and handed it to Mandy, who began to pack it. "Okay, Kelly. Let's try this again. You take care of the head. We'll help get her on her feet."

Everyone took their positions, and on the count of three, Kelly spoke firmly to her horse. "Up you go, Crystal." She applied pressure to the lead rope as she spoke.

The barn was full of grunts as the men applied their strength to rolling her forward. Then they all held their breath as Crystal struggled to get her feet underneath her. The barn erupted in cheers again as she won the fight and surged to her feet. Kelly hugged her neck and steadied her as she stood swaying.

Dr. Shackleford smiled as Granddaddy stepped forward to pump his hand. "Fine job, Doc. I've never seen one come that close to the edge and make it back. Congratulations."

"Thanks, Mr. Porter," smiled Dr. Shackleford. "I don't know that I had a lot to do with it, though. I thought she'd gone too far myself. But I looked outside and saw the Marshalls and Greg praying. I believe that's what turned the tide. Medicine can only do so much. I wouldn't say I'm real religious, but I know it wasn't me that made Crystal well tonight."

Kelly was startled by his words. She had been so absorbed in her own misery that she had not even thought to pray. And she had been completely unaware that her parents and Greg had prayed! Her eyes locked with Peggy's. Kelly felt love flow through her as they exchanged smiles. She noticed the delight on her father's face as well as the grin locked on Greg's. How could one girl be so lucky? Not lucky, she corrected herself. Blessed! Even her hard head was able to recognize God at work.

FIFTEEN

Mr. Shackleford turned to her. "Now the hard work begins, Kelly. It's almost two now. I want Crystal walking for the next four hours, at least. She's not going to like it, but she's going to have to do it. I don't want you to put her up until she's drunk some water and eaten a little food. It may take longer than four hours."

Kelly answered eagerly, "I'll do anything for Crystal. I'm just so glad she's going to be okay. I don't know what I would have done if . . ." Her voice trailed off as she shuddered at the thought of Crystal's close call.

"She's a fine filly, Kelly. One reason she pulled through is because of how well you take care of her. Just give her a little time. I'll come by sometime in the morning to check on her, but don't worry about being here. Once she's eating and drinking, you can put her up. Both of you will be ready for a long rest. We need to get her intestinal system working right again. Then rest is the best medicine. I wouldn't ride her for several days. Take her for long walks, but let her take it easy."

Kelly nodded as the doctor turned to Grand-daddy. "I'd see if you can find out what caused her colic, Mr. Porter. I'd hate to see it happen to more of your animals. There has to be a reason a fine, healthy animal like that would get sick."

"You're right, Doc. We'll check things out now that Crystal is back on her feet. Thanks for coming out. I'm sure you're ready to go home and get some sleep yourself."

The doctor grinned wearily. "Yeah. It's been a long day. But I like the cases with happy endings." With a wave of his hand, he headed for his truck—and home.

Kelly turned back to her filly. Greg picked up the red blanket that had covered her as she lay in the stall and laid it across her back. The night had gotten very cold, and it was still important for her to keep warm. For the first time, Kelly realized she was shivering. Moving around to the side of her horse, she passed the straps underneath to Greg who secured them. Once Crystal was blanketed, Kelly gave a tug on the rope. Crystal shook her head and refused to budge. Taking a firmer hold on the lead line, Kelly spoke decisively to the weary horse.

"I know you're tired, but this is for your own good. Let's go."

Crystal seemed to recognize the determination in her owner's voice. Lowering her head, she heaved a huge sigh and followed Kelly from the stall. Relief surged through Kelly's body. She had been afraid of not being able to get her to move. The droop of Crystal's proud head tore at Kelly's heart. She longed to let Crystal lay down and sleep, but she

A Matter of Trust
203

knew that would be the worst thing for her. Four hours was going to seem like an eternity to Crystal.

"Do you want me to walk her, Kelly?" Greg offered. "You look pretty beat."

"Thanks, but I'd like to start her out. I'm sure I'll be ready for a break soon, but for right now I just want to assure myself she's okay."

Greg smiled and nodded his head. "I understand. I'll walk with you. When you get tired, I'll take over for a while."

"We'll all take turns walking her," Kelly's dad spoke up. "We're in this for the long haul. None of us are going to be willing to leave until Crystal's okay to put up."

Kelly looked around and was overwhelmed with the love of the people surrounding her. Once again, she locked eyes with Peggy and smiled. They would have time to talk later. It was enough to know the walls had come down.

"You know," her father continued, "I hate to admit my ignorance, but other than seeing that colic can be fatal, I know nothing about it. What happened here tonight?"

"Go ahead and start walking Crystal, Kelly," Mandy smiled. "I'll explain to your father and Peggy."

Kelly nodded and headed down the aisle with Greg. She could hear Mandy talking as they walked Crystal up and down the long corridor.

"When a horse colics," Mandy began, "it's really like a huge case of indigestion. The problem with horses is that they have no way to throw up and get rid of whatever is causing them to be sick. Their indigestion causes gas to build up in their stomachs. That's why Crystal looked so swollen and bloated. She still does, but that will eventually go away. A lot of things can cause it—sudden changes in feed, overeating, exhaustion and fatigue, too much water before a hot horse cools off, bad teeth, or bad feed."

Kelly's mind raced as she listened to Mandy's voice. As she thought about it, she decided the problem must be the feed. Nothing else seemed to make sense.

"We tried hard to get Crystal up on her feet when we first found her," Mandy continued. "Once a horse lies down, they will start rolling and thrashing around to try to get rid of the pain. Their movements can cause the stomach to get all twisted, which can lead to rupture and hemorrhage. We had a horse die two years ago. We didn't find him until it was too late."

Kelly shivered as she considered once more what could have happened. She murmured quietly to her exhausted filly, thankful that Crystal had pulled through.

"Anyway, now that she's up, the very best thing is to keep her moving," Mandy added. "It will help her circulation and get the gas moving out. Once all the gas has been expelled and the bloating is gone, it will be safe to let her lie down and sleep. Oftentimes, in cases where it isn't as serious as Crystal's, the vet will put a stomach tube in to release the gases and flush out the stomach. Since Crystal had already gone into shock, he had to go straight to antibiotics in order to stabilize her and bring her around."

Finishing her explanation, Mandy moved in the direction of the feed room. "I'm going to take a look at the feed. That's the only reasonable culprit I can come up with. Excuse me."

Kelly continued to walk up and down the aisle. Her father motioned to Greg, and they disappeared outside, reappearing a few minutes later with hay bales. They made a couple of more trips until they had a hay bale for each person to sit on or lean against.

"If we're going to be here all night, we might as well be comfortable," her father said cheerfully.

Granddaddy turned to Peggy. "I'm going to call it a night. This old body can't take these all-nighters. Why don't you come in and make yourself at home in my kitchen? I'm sure everyone would appreciate some coffee or hot chocolate."

"Something hot to drink would be wonderful, Granddaddy," Peggy said. "I'm sure everyone is chilled. Kelly is still shaking."

Granddaddy looked at Kelly and smiled. "I've got some coveralls that will keep her warm. She may not look like a beauty queen, but I guarantee she'll quit shaking."

"I've discovered the culprit," Mandy announced when she returned. "It was a moldy bag of feed. I guess it's my fault. I ran out of feed just as I got to Crystal. She was the last horse, so I just opened the bag and scooped out her ration. I didn't check it very closely. The barn was pretty dark. Kelly, I'm sorry." Mandy's voice was full of remorse.

Kelly hastened to reassure her friend. "It's not your fault, Mandy. Anyone could have made that mistake. Lots of us have done the same thing before. I bet we won't anymore, though. Anyway, she's going to be fine."

Mandy sighed in relief. "I never would have forgiven myself if something had happened to your horse."

"The rest of the night is going to be pretty routine, Mandy," Kelly's dad said gently. "We seem to just have a lot of walking ahead of us. The rest of us can go home when this is all over. You have a full day of classes tomorrow. Why don't you go on to bed? We'll come get you if anything happens. There are plenty of us here to walk Crystal."

Mandy hesitated and then smiled gratefully. "My heart wants to stay, but my mind and my body have to agree with you. I'm going to turn in. *Please* let me know if anything happens. I'm a light sleeper, so I won't be hard to wake."

"We will, Mandy," Kelly spoke quickly. "Go get some sleep. And don't worry about my classes tomorrow. I'm sure I can survive until lunch with no sleep. Now that I know Crystal is going to be okay, I'm fine. I can crash after classes are done."

Kelly saw her father start to protest, but he stopped when Peggy touched his arm and shook her head. Kelly's heart once more flooded with love and gratitude. Peggy knew how she felt. Peggy had always known how she felt.

Mandy nodded and moved from the barn. Kelly walked Crystal for another thirty minutes before Greg took the rope from her hand and ordered her to sit down for a while.

"I'm perfectly capable of walking up and down the aisle," he said. "I think Crystal has decided it's walk time whether she likes it or not. She's kind of slipped into the robot stage. She doesn't act like she's awake, but her feet keep moving. If you don't sit down for a while, you're going to be the same way. Now sit!"

Kelly walked over to a hay bale and sat.

Her father laughed out loud. "I knew I liked you, Greg. Anyone who can order this hardheaded female around is tops in my book!"

Kelly made a face but had to admit it felt good to relax against the hay bale. She looked up and smiled as Peggy walked over and sank down beside her. Peggy sensed she was too tired to talk. Putting her arm around Kelly, Peggy pulled her close and let her lay her head on her chest. Kelly was awed at the peace she felt. Within minutes she was asleep.

The next thing Kelly knew, Peggy was shaking her gently. "Kelly. Time to wake up. Your father is here with some food."

Groggily she opened her eyes. Seeing the faint light of dawn creeping across the sky outside the barn, she sat up. "What time is it? How long have I been asleep? How is Crystal?"

Greg laughed. "One question at a time, sleeping beauty. It's almost six. You've been asleep about three hours, and Crystal just took her first drink of water. I thought you would want to celebrate with us."

Kelly sprung up and moved toward her filly. "I've been asleep for three hours? Who has been walking Crystal? Why did you let me sleep so long?"

"You are full of questions this morning, aren't you?" laughed Greg. "Yes, you've been asleep for three hours. We decided that if you were determined to teach classes today, we were determined you would get some sleep. Your father, Peggy, and I have taken turns walking Crystal."

"And she just drank water? Has she eaten anything yet?"

"I haven't offered her feed yet. She needed to drink first. She seems thirsty, but I'm only letting her have a little at a time. Her stomach needs to make a slow adjustment. Why don't you take her and see if she wants to eat something?"

Kelly reached for the lead rope and was overjoyed to see that life had returned to Crystal's eyes. It was obvious she was tired, but the spark was back. Leading her into the stall, Kelly offered her the fresh feed someone, probably Greg, had placed there while she was sleeping. Delight surged through her as Crystal took several small mouthfuls.

"I'd say the doctor's orders have been met," Greg happily proclaimed. "Four hours were up twenty minutes ago. I think your filly has earned a well-deserved rest. Your father just showed up with food. Let's eat. I'm starving!" Greg patted his stomach. "I don't think you can colic from starvation, but I wouldn't want to test the theory any longer."

Kelly laughed, gave her horse a final hug and kiss, and then carefully closed the stall door. Turning, she followed Greg down the corridor and out to the clubhouse where her father and Peggy were unpacking sandwiches, chips, and cookies. There were also two thermos bottles full of hot chocolate and coffee. Silence reigned as the hungry crew dug into the food before them. Kelly was aware of a deep peace permeating the room. Looking around, she was filled with thankfulness for these people who loved her and who had stood with her. She wanted them to know.

"I don't know how to thank all of you," Kelly began hesitantly, trying to express her feelings. "You were so wonderful. I appreciate all you did so much."

Greg and her father nodded. Peggy walked over and gave her a hug. Kelly hugged her back. She knew she could never get enough of Peggy's warm hugs.

When everyone finished their sandwiches, Greg caught Kelly's eye and asked, "Want to go for a walk?"

"Sure. But do *you* want to go for a walk? Haven't you had enough?"

Greg laughed. "Oh, I don't plan on a long walk. I just have something I want to show you."

Curious, Kelly accepted the hand he extended and followed him outside. Side by side they walked to Crystal's stall. Peering inside, she saw her filly had already lain down and was sound asleep. She smiled at Greg and then walked on as he tugged at her hand. Moving through the doors, they walked over to the pasture gate.

"Wait for a few minutes. You'll see what I want to show you."

Kelly wrapped her arms across the gate and waited. She was thrilled when Greg stepped up behind her and wrapped his arms around her waist. Lowering her arms, she settled back into his embrace. They stood that way for several minutes, and then she took a deep breath of delight. As she watched, the golden orb of the sun broke over the horizon, casting a tawny hue on the world. The clouds hovering low in the sky took on deep shades of rose and purple.

"A new day and a new beginning, Kelly. You've changed since last night. What is it?"

Kelly leaned back in his arms and spoke softly. "I think I finally quit running. I hadn't realized it before, but now I know I never dealt with my feelings about my mom's death. All the grief was locked up inside. It hurt so much that I was scared to let anyone else get too close. I was afraid of losing someone again. I wasn't sure I could deal with more pain. I had put up some of those walls Martin has been talking about the last few weeks, and I didn't want to let them down. But lately they've been battered pretty hard. First I was afraid that Emily was dead, and then Crystal almost died. I know now that God was allowing all that to break down my walls. All I knew last night was that I was tired and couldn't do it on my own anymore. When Peggy grabbed me and wouldn't let me go, I just decided to quit fighting. I don't understand it all yet. I just know I feel a great release inside, and it feels really good."

Greg hugged her close. "I'm so glad, Kelly. Even though you're tired, I can see the change. It never ceases to amaze me how God works in our lives. Only God could make something good come from Crystal almost dying."

Kelly nodded and looked back at the splendid sunrise. "I think you said it best. A new day and a new beginning."

She was expecting the tender kiss he gave her

when he turned her in his arms to face him.

• • •

Kelly was exhausted as she settled into her window seat, but she wasn't ready to go to sleep yet. She was sure Peggy would be up to check on her, and she wanted to be awake so they could talk.

The day had been long, but Kelly had found the energy to do everything. Her classes had gone well that morning, Greg had brought her some lunch, and then together they had walked Crystal for an hour around the pastures and down by the lake. Crystal wasn't her old self yet, but the spring was back in her step, and she seemed curious to know what all the concern was for.

Kelly relaxed against the seat, content with her world. A light tap sounded on the door.

"Come in."

Peggy smiled when she saw Kelly in her favorite spot. "Can't sleep?"

"I was waiting for you."

Peggy smiled again and walked across the room to join her. Kelly moved to make room. They sat in silence for a few moments, and then Kelly spoke.

"About last night...I'm really sorry for the things I said. I didn't mean them. I was just upset."

Peggy nodded. "I know. It's okay."

"No. It's not okay. But I know you forgive me, and I'm glad. I was being pretty stupid."

"All of us are stupid at some point in our lives."

"Yeah, well I seem to have more than my fair share of times." Kelly paused. "Thank you for holding on to me last night. I've done a lot of thinking today and understand a lot more of why I've acted the way I have. I didn't know what to do with you, Peggy. I had never let go of my mom, so there just wasn't room for you. When Crystal almost died, I was finally able to look at all the pain and let it go. And I had so many walls up. I didn't want to love you and risk losing someone again. I thought it was easier to stay behind my walls but Martin is right—it's a pretty lonely place. I'll never forget my mom, but I know I need you, too." Kelly stopped talking and didn't know what else to say.

Peggy saved her from having to come up with something. She did the very best thing. She simply opened her arms and wrapped them around Kelly. "We'll have plenty of time to work out our relationship. Right now I'm just glad that you've quit fighting God. That's who has really been knocking down your walls. I'll do my best to always be here for you, Kelly. I love you very much. But I'm human, and sometimes I'll let you down. God is the only one who will always be there and always do the right thing. There will come times in the future when you'll think you need to go back behind your walls because someone will do something to hurt you. That's when you have to run to God and let him take care of your heart and your hurt. You're right, though. Walls make your life a very lonely place."

Kelly nodded drowsily. They sat in silence for several minutes. She was only vaguely aware of being led across the floor and tucked into bed.

That night, Kelly's dreams were filled with happy images of Crystal, Greg, her mother, Emily, her dad . . . and Peggy.

SIXTEEN

Kelly could scarcely believe a month had passed since Crystal's bout with colic. It had been a month full of school, fun, and lots of time at the stables. Jason had actually become a gentleman and now was owned by one of Granddaddy's regulars. Crystal acted like she had never been sick. She was rambunctious and learning new things faster than ever. Every weekend had been full of fun activities as she and Greg became closer friends with Brent and Julie. And things at home were great. She and Peggy were drawing closer and closer through their late-night talks on the window seat.

"Penny for your thoughts."

Kelly laughed at Greg's remark. They were heading back to the barn after a long ride. Granddaddy always called off classes on Thanksgiving weekend to encourage families to spend time together. Kelly and Greg had come out and spent hours exploring the countryside. They were headed back home so they would have plenty of time to get ready for the

church's Thanksgiving Family Picnic that afternoon. The weather was perfect. It was crisp and
cool, but dry.

"I don't think a penny will touch them. Maybe a
dollar."

"Whoa! Must be some pretty heavy thoughts."

"I don't know about heavy, but they are definitely
good," Kelly smiled. "I'm just thinking about everything that has happened this fall. I thought that
when I became a Christian, all my problems would
go away. It was quite a blow to discover I was still
having problems and still making stupid mistakes.
My blunders with Peggy are classic examples. It's
neat, though, to see how God was working in my life
the whole time—even when I didn't know it. I've
learned a lot. And I know I have a lot to learn. I've
been reading every night in my Bible. I think I'm
finally getting the idea of what it means to give God
your whole life. I thought I'd arrived when I asked
him to come into my life. Now I know it was just the
beginning step."

"You're right," Greg nodded his head in agreement. "Those are worth a dollar!" He laughed and
then became serious. "It's neat to see how much
you've grown, Kelly. I thought you were great before—now you're something else."

Kelly blushed but smiled over at him. Their relationship was still a thrill to her. She couldn't imagine
it being anything else. He hadn't kissed her again
since that morning by the gate, but it didn't matter.
She knew how much he liked her. She was happy
with holding hands and long hugs. His kisses, when
they happened, were special memories to treasure.

She would hate to think they would ever become commonplace. And she would hate for them to cause a problem in their relationship.

"You're a big reason why I've come as far as I have," Kelly said honestly. "I really appreciate your friendship. I was thinking about you Thursday when we were going around the dinner table talking about what we are thankful for. I'm glad you're my boyfriend, but I'm even more glad you're my friend."

• • •

Kelly and her family piled out of the car as they got to the grounds of the Sheltons' estate, Deerfield Farm. The Sheltons had offered to let the church have the picnic there. It was a perfect location with plenty of open fields for play and lots of tree-covered areas for picnic blankets to be spread. Greg and his parents pulled in behind the Marshalls' car with Julie, Brent, and their parents not far behind. They had all met at Greg's house and caravanned over.

Kelly joined her three friends in helping set up their site—laying out blankets, setting up chairs, and bringing out the picnic baskets. Finally, Peggy shooed them away.

"I'll do the last little bit. Y'all go have fun. You only have a couple of hours to play before dinner."

"What are you going to do, Peggy?" Kelly asked.

"I'm not sure. I can assure you, though, that at some point your father and I will make our way down to the volleyball court. You better go warm up so we don't beat your team too bad!"

The four friends made rounds of all the games and activities scattered around the area. Volleyball was their favorite, so they eventually settled down at the volleyball pit. That was where they were when the bell clanged for dinner. In moments, they all converged on their picnic area.

Emily had brought two friends from school, and Kelly's parents had invited a family from work, so their area was full of talk and laughter. Peggy had been right to coordinate the preparation of so much food. There were plates of fried chicken, platters of deviled eggs, coleslaw, homemade bread, pickles, and fresh applesauce. To finish it all off, Peggy had made an angel food cake with fresh strawberries and Cool Whip to top it.

Everyone had just finished consuming the mountain of food when Chad Stevens, the pastor of Kingsport Community Church, strode to the mike resting on the temporary platform erected for the picnic.

"I see most of you are finished eating," he said with a smile, "so I'd like to begin our traditional time of sharing family memories. Today's world is a tough place to be a family. There is a lot going against us. Divorce rates are sky high, and many marriages are under attack. A lot of mothers have to work, even though they would much rather be at home. But you know, families are God's special plan, and he will help us protect them if we really want to. I know there have been many great things that have happened this year in families. Who would like to share first?"

Pastor Stevens moved aside as Joe Campbell, a man Kelly only knew by name, stepped forward.

"This year has been a hard one *and* a good one," he began. "About ten months ago, my wife, Carol, and I were planning on getting a divorce. We just couldn't seem to make our marriage work. We fought all the time. We were making ourselves and our kids miserable. We met over dinner one night to call it quits, and we spent our time fighting over who would get the kids. During that talk, miraculously, we decided we would try it again. We later found out that a group of people had met to pray for us that night. We started counseling and finally began to understand each other. The last three months have been wonderful. I love Carol more than ever, and our kids know they have a home for keeps."

Everyone clapped as Joe walked from the platform.

"Wow!" Greg commented. "That took a lot of courage to say all that in front of so many people."

Kelly nodded in agreement.

Joe's place was taken by Eric Ward, a warm and funny man whom Kelly liked a lot. He played golf with her father sometimes. She wondered what he had to share.

"Our family had a very special thing happen this year. Many of you know that my wife, Elaine, and I have five kids. What most of you don't know is that we actually have six." Mr. Ward paused a moment, and Kelly could tell he was getting choked up. "When Elaine and I were in high school and dating, we made some mistakes, and Elaine ended up pregnant. We considered abortion, but it wasn't as accepted back then as it is now—thank God! Elaine decided to have the baby, and we gave it up for adoption. We didn't get married until four years later, when I finished college. We always wondered what happened to the baby, but we were never able to find out. Two months ago we received a phone call from our first daughter! She turned eighteen last year and found us with the help of her adoptive parents. This summer she came and spent two weeks with us. I can't begin to describe the joy God gave us by reuniting us with our other daughter. She has wonderful parents who love her very much, and we will always be grateful they were willing to share her with us for a while."

The clapping was enthusiastic as Mr. Ward left the stage. Kelly could only stare in amazement. This God she had hooked up with was pretty amazing. She was beginning to understand that he truly was in the business of rebuilding lives and offering new starts for everyone.

A woman stood and moved forward. Kelly knew her name was Rachel Morris. She had heard stories about her. She was curious to hear what she would say.

"Hi," Mrs. Morris said shyly. "Many of you know my husband committed suicide two years ago. His business was failing, and he had lost all hope. He didn't see any other way out of the mess, I guess. The last two years have been rough for myself and my four kids, but I'm standing up to say thank you to this church for being so much of a family for us. Thank you to everyone here who loved me and supported me during that time. I especially want to thank the men who stepped forward to be a father to my kids. We still have hard times, but I know we're not alone. This church is a family for us, and I just want you to know how much we appreciate it."

Kelly rubbed tears from her eyes when Mrs. Morris stopped speaking. She couldn't even imagine what it would be like to have to go through something like that. Greg reached over for her hand. She turned her face and saw tears glistening in his eyes as well.

Several more families stood up to share, and then Kelly was surprised to see her own father head for the mike. Scott Marshall smiled as he turned around to face the crowd.

"Most of you know my wife died of cancer several years ago. For five years it was just me and my two daughters, Kelly and Emily. We were a happy family, but I have to admit I was lonely. Then God brought Peggy Sanders into my life. She not only agreed to become my wife, but she also introduced me to a life in Jesus Christ. I had gone to church before but had never really understood what making Jesus your Lord was all about. Since then, both of my kids have become Christians, and our family has become even more of a precious thing to me. Some of the adjustments we had to make were tough, but God has been faithful, and the four of us have truly become a family. It constantly amazes me to see the things God will do in a family if we will allow Him to work in our lives."

Kelly was proud of her father as he moved back to their area. The entire group bowed their heads as Pastor Stevens led them in a final prayer.

The picnic coordinator moved to the mike. "There will be hayrides going out in ten minutes.

That should give all of you enough time to clear away your food and meet us at the wagons next to the bonfire."

Kelly and Greg pitched in to help with the cleanup and then joined their families next to the wagons. The tractor-drawn wagons were huge, but it took five of them to accommodate everyone. Greg drew Kelly laughing into the hay. Kelly then saw her father and Peggy looking for a wagon to join. Leaning out from the hay, Kelly called and beckoned to them. Smiling, they walked over, jumped onto the wagon, and settled down next to them. Kelly felt a deep contentment as she relaxed in the love surrounding her. Everyone snuggled down into the hay, grateful for its warmth against the chill of the night. Singing filled the air as first one wagon, and then another, started songs.

About the Author

Ginny Williams grew up loving and working with horses. When she got older, she added a love for teenagers to the top of her list. She admits she goes through withdrawal when she doesn't have kids around her, not that that has happened much in her fifteen years of youth ministry.

Ginny lives on a large farm outside of Richmond, Virginia, with her husband, Louis, two Labrador retrievers, a large flock of Canada geese, and a herd of deer. When she's not writing or speaking to youth groups, she can be found using her degree in recreation. She loves to travel and play. She bikes, plays tennis, windsurfs, rides horses (of course!), plays softball—she'll do anything that's fun! She's planning a bike trip across the country, and she's waiting for her chance to skydive and bungee jump.

**Capturing the Spirit
of the Next Generation...**

The Class of 2000
by Ginny Williams

Second Chances

At 15 years old, Kelly finds her life in sudden turmoil when her widowed father decides to remarry. Struggling with bitter feelings, Kelly determines that she'll never accept her father's wife. But a beautiful black horse, a special friend, and a daring rescue from a burning barn give Kelly a different perspective on those she loves...and a chance to start over with her new stepmother.

A Matter of Trust

God changed Kelly's heart, but now she's finding it difficult sometimes for her actions to follow. Conflict at home threatens to tear the family apart. But when her beloved horse almost dies, Kelly discovers strength and support from an unlikely source—her stepmom.

Lost-and-Found Friend

Kelly's friend Brent is a very sensitive, very intense person who is adept at hiding his troubles. When pressures at home become overwhelming, Brent attempts suicide. Concerned friends, a ski trip, and a life-threatening snowstorm help Brent realize there are alternative ways to solve his problems.